In the Grip of Winter

The first signs were not good for wild creatures as the old year drew to a close. December came in with a blizzard, and over the next few weeks a cruel, bitter frost held the Park in its grip night after night. During the daylight hours the sun gleamed fitfully but snow clouds blotted it out for most of the day, and so very little of the frost disappeared. The ground became as hard as iron, and ice coated the Edible Frogs' pond to a thickness of two inches.

By the same author:
The Ram of Sweetriver
The King of the Vagabonds
The City Cats
The Beach Dogs
Just Nuffin
A Great Escape
A Legacy of Ghosts

The Farthing Wood Series:

Animals of Farthing Wood
In the Grip of Winter
Fox's Feud
Fox Cub Bold
The Siege of White Deer Park
In the Path of the Storm
Battle for the Park

In the Grip of Winter

Colin Dann

Illustrated by Terry Riley

RED FOX

A Red Fox Book

Published by Random House Children's Books
20 Vauxhall Bridge Road, London SW1V 2SA

A division of Random House UK Ltd

London Melbourne Sydney Auckland
Johannesburg and agencies throughout the world

First published by Hutchinson 1981
Sparrow edition 1982
Beaver reprint 1985, 1987 (twice)
1988 (three times) and 1989 (twice)
Red Fox edition 1990
Reprinted 1991, 1992
This edition 1992

9 10 8

Printed and bound in Great Britain by Clays Ltd, St Ives PLC

RANDOM HOUSE UK Limited Reg. No. 954009

ISBN 0 09 920511 4

The Random House Group Limited supports The Forest Stewardship
Council (FSC®), the leading international forest certification organisation.
Our books carrying the FSC label are printed on FSC® certified paper.
FSC is the only forest certification scheme endorsed by the leading
environmental organisations, including Greenpeace. Our
paper procurement policy can be found at
www.randomhouse.co.uk/environment

Contents

For Kathy

1
First Signs

It was soon time for the animals and birds to face their
first winter in White Deer Park. They had moved in a
group from their old homes in Farthing Wood when it
was destroyed by Man, and the strong links of friendship
and the spirit of community forged during their long
journey had caused them to build their new homes close
to one another. So a certain corner of the White Deer
Park Nature Reserve became almost a new Farthing
Wood for them, and every creature found conditions
exactly right for his particular requirements.

In the centre of this area lay the Hollow which, from
their earliest arrival in the Park, had formed their
meeting-place. In the autumn months they met less often
and, eventually, as the evenings grew colder, both Adder

and Toad knew it was time for them to go underground for the winter.

It was late October when Adder ceased to lie in wait at the edge of the Edible Frogs' pond, a feat of patience that had not brought him its hoped-for reward. 'This cool weather makes me feel so sleepy,' he remarked to Toad, whom he sometimes saw going for a swim.

'Me too,' replied Toad. 'I've been busy fattening up while food is still available. I must confess that now I really feel ready for a nice long snooze.'

'Where will you go?' Adder enquired.

'Oh, hereabouts. The earth is soft in this bank and I've noticed quite a few holes remaining that must have been dug in earlier years.'

'Mmm,' Adder mused. 'That would suit me admirably. Those frogs would then have the benefit of my presence in spirit throughout the winter.'

Toad chuckled. 'I'm sure they won't be aware of it,' he said. 'They're digging themselves into the mud on the pond bottom. Once they've settled, they'll be quite oblivious of everything.'

'I shall, too,' admitted the snake. 'My only interest at the moment is in sleep.'

'Er – have you made your farewells?' Toad asked him hesitantly.

'Farewells? Stuff and nonsense!' Adder rasped. 'No-one cares to seek me out when I'm around, so they'll hardly miss me when I'm not.'

Toad felt embarrassed. 'Oh, I don't know,' he said awkwardly. 'I think it's just that most of us feel you prefer to be alone.'

'I *do*,' said Adder a little too quickly, as if trying to dispel any doubts at all about the matter. 'However, Toad, I've no objection to your company,' he added not uncourteously.

'Thank you, Adder. Er – when do you plan to begin hibernation?'

'Straight away, of course. No point in hanging around above ground in these sort of temperatures.'

'If you can wait until tomorrow I'll join you,' Toad suggested. 'Just leave me time to call on Fox and Badger, and Owl, perhaps.'

'Oh, I can't sit here waiting for the frost to bite me while you go making social visits,' said Adder impatiently. 'I'm going underground tonight.'

'Very well,' said Toad. 'As you wish. But I really don't see what difference one more day would make.'

Adder made a gesture. 'I'll tell you what,' he offered. 'Let's choose a comfortable hole now, and then you'll know where to find me.'

Toad considered this was about the closest Adder was ever likely to come to being companionable, so he accepted readily.

Having chosen the best site, Adder promptly disappeared into the earth with a hastily lisped, 'Try not to wake me.' Toad wryly shook his head and set off to find his friends.

As he approached the Hollow, the sky was darkening fast, and a cold wind was whipping through the grass. Toad almost wished he had followed Adder into the shelter of the hole, but he felt he just could not have been so unfriendly. No movement could be discerned in or around the Hollow, so Toad sat down to wait, amusing himself by flicking up a stray beetle here and there. Presently a ghostly form could be seen lumbering towards him through the gloom. Toad made out Badger's grey outline.

'Hallo, my dear friend,' said Badger warmly. 'I'm surprised to see you out on a cold night like this.'

'It'll be the last time,' commented Toad. 'Before the Spring.'

'I see, I see,' Badger nodded. 'You've come to say goodbye. Well, it could be for quite some time, you know.' He paused and snuffled in the brisk air.

'Do you think it will be a hard winter?' Toad asked.

'Every winter is hard for some,' Badger answered. 'The weakest among us always suffer the most. The small creatures: the mice, the shrews, the voles and, particularly, the small birds – every winter takes its toll of them. But yes – I sense that this winter will be one to reckon with. There's something in that wind. . . .'

'I felt it, too,' Toad nodded. 'And Adder – he's already settled.'

'Just like him to disappear without trace,' Badger muttered. 'Well, at least it'll put an end to that nonsense of his with the Edible Frogs.'

'Yes, until next year,' Toad remarked drily. 'But, d'you know, Badger, he actually invited me to join him in his sleeping quarters – at least, in a roundabout sort of way.'

'Oh, he's all right really,' Badger granted. 'After all, you can't expect a great deal of warm feeling from a snake.'

While they were talking, they saw Fox and Vixen slip stealthily past in the moonlight, intent upon hunting. Toad was disappointed. 'They could have stopped for a word,' he complained, 'when I've made a point of coming to see you all. And in this wind, too.'

'Don't feel slighted, old friend,' Badger said earnestly. 'I'm sure they don't realize you're about to go underground. It wouldn't be like Fox.'

'No, I suppose not,' Toad assented. 'But he's not the close friend he used to be before Vixen came – at least not to me. Ah well, that's the feminine influence for you.'

Badger nodded his striped head, smiling gently. 'We old bachelors have little experience of such things, I'm afraid,' he said softly. 'We live out our solitary lives in rather a narrow way by comparison.'

Toad was touched by the note of wistfulness in Badger's voice. 'I – I never realized you felt that way about it, Badger,' he said in a low croak. 'But there are lady badgers in the park, surely?'

'Oh yes, it's different from Farthing Wood in that respect,' Badger agreed. 'But I've been living alone for too long now. I couldn't adjust.'

Toad was silent. He felt it was best not to add anything. There was a long pause and Toad shuffled a trifle uncomfortably. 'Hallo,' he said suddenly, 'here's another old bachelor,' as Tawny Owl fluttered to the ground beside them.

Owl nodded to them both, then said, 'I hope you weren't speaking derisively, Toad. I can't answer for you two, but I'm single from choice alone.'

'*Your* choice – or the choice of the lady owls?' Toad asked innocently. Badger muffled a laugh.

'Very amusing, I'm sure,' Owl snorted. 'I'd better go. I didn't come here to be insulted.'

Badger, so often the peacemaker, stepped in. 'Now, Owl, don't be so hasty. No offence was intended. Toad's come to see us because he's going into hibernation soon.'

'Humph!' Tawny Owl grunted, ruffling his feathers. But he did not go.

'Yes, tomorrow to be exact,' Toad informed him. 'And I shan't be sorry. I sympathize with you fellows who have to face whatever comes: ice, frost or snow. It's marvellous just to fall asleep and forget all about it – and then, simply wake up as soon as it's warm again.'

'There's certainly a lot to be said for it,' Badger remarked.

'But it takes months off your life,' Tawny Owl pointed out. 'You may as well be dead for six months of the year.'

'Not quite as long as that,' Toad corrected him. 'Anyway, it depends on the weather. In a mild winter, I might be out again in February.'

'Mark my words, Toad,' Tawny Owl said with emphasis. 'This is going to be a difficult one.'

'Then my heartfelt good wishes go with you,' Toad said sincerely. 'I hope you all come through.'

The three friends remained talking a while longer, while the cold wind continued to blow. Finally Tawny Owl declared he was hungry and flew off in search of prey. Something struck Toad at his departure and he fell to musing.

'You know, Badger,' he said presently, 'we shake our heads over old Adder and his designs on my cousins the frogs, but really he's not so much a threat to the denizens of White Deer Park as Fox or Owl, who go hunting here every night.'

'A thought that had also occurred to me,' Badger acknowledged. 'But there were foxes and owls – and other predators – in the park before we arrived. So in the same way the voles and fieldmice and rabbits of the Farthing Wood party run the same risk from the enemies already here.'

Toad nodded and sighed. 'My idea of the Nature Reserve as a new and safe home for all has not proved quite true,' he said ruefully.

'Nowhere is completely safe,' Badger assured him. 'But the Park is about as safe as anywhere could be for wild creatures, for there is no presence of Man. And in that respect it is a veritable haven compared with Farthing Wood.'

Toad grinned. 'You've soothed my mind as usual,' he

said. 'Well, Badger, I shall not delay you any longer. Farewell till Spring.' He turned to make his way back to the bank where Adder was already asleep. On his way he encountered Fox again. This time Fox stopped. Toad explained where he was going.

'You could perhaps give a message to Adder for me,' Fox requested. 'Tell him to go down deep. And you too, Toad,' he finished enigmatically.

'How deep?' queried Toad.

'As deep as it takes to escape the frost.' Fox shivered in the wind as if illustrating his warning.

'We shall take heed, Fox,' Toad answered. 'Have no fear.'

They parted and Toad crawled on towards his objective. Fox stood and watched him a long time. Then he shook himself vigorously and went to rejoin Vixen. Winter, he knew, was hovering just around the corner, waiting to pounce.

2

First Snow

During the next few weeks, as October passed into November and the leaves fell thick and fast in White Deer Park, the animals kept very much to themselves. Their main preoccupation was food.

Nature had provided an abundance of berries and nuts which, as all wild creatures know, is a sure sign of severe weather to come. So the squirrels and the voles and the fieldmice were able to feast themselves for a short period. There was a spell of heavy rain which brought out the slugs and worms, and Hedgehog and his friends fattened themselves up nicely before they made their winter homes under thick piles of leaves and brush in the undergrowth. As they disappeared to hibernate, the other animals knew that time was running out, and renewed their efforts. All ate well for a space.

The first heavy frost descended at the end of November and Mole, whose tremendous appetite was undimmed, found an abundance of earthworms deep underground. Their movements were restricted by the frozen ground near the surface and he amassed a large collection against emergencies. He was so proud of his efforts that he was bursting to tell someone about them. So he tunnelled his way through to Badger's set which was close by, and woke him from a late afternoon snooze.

'It's me! Mole!' he cried unnecessarily. 'Wake up, Badger. I want to tell you what I've been doing.'

Badger sat up slowly and sniffed at his small friend. 'You smell of worms,' he said abruptly.

'Of course I do,' Mole replied importantly. 'I've been harvesting them.'

'Harvesting them?'

'Yes, you know, collecting – er – gathering them. I've never known it to be so easy to catch so many. They're all securely stowed away in a nice big pile of earth where my nest is.'

'I didn't realize it was possible to stow away slippery things like worms,' Badger remarked. 'By the time you get back they'll all have wriggled away.'

'Oh no, they won't,' declared Mole. 'They can't,' he added mysteriously.

'Why, what have you done to them?'

'I've tied them up in knots!' cried Mole excitedly. 'And they can't undo themselves.' He began to giggle as he saw Badger's stupefied expression, and he was still giggling when Badger received another guest, in the shape of Fox.

'Have you been outside?' he asked, after greeting them.

They shook their heads.

'It's snowing,' he stated.

They followed him up Badger's exit tunnel to look. It was dusk, but the sloping ground in the little copse Badger had favoured as his new home was gleaming white. The trees themselves glowed mysteriously in their soft new clothing. They watched the large flat flakes drift silently downward. There was no wind. Everything seemed completely still save what was dropping steadily from the sky.

'It's already quite thick,' Fox told them. 'I can't see my tracks.'

'I've never seen snow falling before,' Mole said as he watched with fascination. His eyes, used to darkness, blinked rapidly in the brightness of the white carpet spread before them. 'Will it cover everything?'

'Not quite everything,' answered Badger. 'But it makes movement very difficult for small creatures. The birds don't have to worry, of course. Except in so far as feeding is concerned.'

'I can only remember one winter in Farthing Wood when it snowed,' said Fox. 'That was when I was very young. But there was only a light fall, and it didn't really hamper anyone's movements.'

'Oh yes,' nodded Badger. 'Of latter years there's not been a great deal of bad weather. But I recall the times when Winter meant Winter, and we had snow every year. Of course, my memory goes farther back than yours, Fox.'

Fox smiled slightly. He knew Badger loved to indulge in reminiscences, and he was aware of his proneness to exaggerate about 'life in the old days'.

'I remember one winter in particular,' Badger continued, delighted to have an audience. 'You hadn't appeared on the scene then, either of you, and I'm pretty certain Tawny Owl wasn't around at that time either.

Anyway, the snow lay on the ground for months, and I had to dig a regular track through it for foraging purposes. Everything was frozen hard – the pond, the stream, every small puddle. My father was still alive then and he taught us how to munch the snow for water. Otherwise we couldn't have drunk and we should have died.'

'What does it taste like? What does it taste like?' shrilled Mole.

'Oh, well – er – like water, I suppose,' replied Badger. 'Yes, and I shall never forget the number of birds and small creatures who perished from the cold.'

'Oh dear, oh dear!' Mole cried. 'I hope you don't mean moles?'

'Well, possibly not moles,' said Badger hurriedly. 'Mostly songbirds really. They couldn't find enough to eat and, naturally, their little bodies weren't able to withstand the bitter weather.'

'Poor things,' said Mole in a subdued tone. 'It's a pity they can't hibernate like Adder and Toad.'

The snow seemed to fall more thickly as they watched. Mole shivered.

'Go back inside,' the kindly Badger said at once. 'It's warm in my sleeping-chamber.'

'I'm not cold,' Mole told him, 'but thank you, Badger. No, it's just the eeriness that made me shiver. It's so quiet and still – it's uncanny.'

Through the ghostly trees they spotted a dark figure stepping through the snow. They all knew at once it was the Warden of the Nature Reserve on his rounds. They watched him stop periodically by a tree and tie something on to a low-hanging branch.

'What's he doing?' Mole asked, whose short-sightedness could only distinguish a tall blur of movement.

'I don't know for sure,' answered Badger. 'But it's my

guess he's leaving some sort of food for the birds.'

'Then that's bad news for us,' Fox said at once. 'Humans never do such things without a particular reason. It is well-known they can tell in advance what sort of weather is approaching. We must be in for some severe times.' He trotted over to look at the objects the Warden had left behind.

'You're right, Badger,' he called back. 'It *is* bird food. Nuts and fat and so on. I hope our feathered friends are up early,' he continued to himself, 'otherwise Squirrel and his pals will be having a feast at their expense.' He said as much to Badger on his return.

'Well, we must stop them,' said that thoughtful animal resolutely. 'The squirrels have buried enough acorns and beech-nuts to feed the whole of White Deer Park.'

'You'll be asleep when *they* get up,' Fox reminded him with a smile. 'You'd better leave it to me to have a word.'

'Will you and Vixen be warm enough in your den?' Badger asked suddenly. 'I've collected plenty of extra bedding for my set, and you're welcome to share it.'

'You're very kind,' replied Fox, 'but I think we're all right. We keep each other warm, you know,' he added.

Badger smiled. 'That must be a great comfort,' he remarked. He looked around. 'Well, I feel like a bit of a ramble. Coming, Fox?'

'With pleasure. Er – see you later, Mole?'

'No, I'll go back to my nest,' said the little animal. 'I'm sure to feel peckish again soon – you know what I'm like.'

'We do indeed,' laughed Fox. 'Shall we go, Badger?'

The two friends ambled off through the snowy wood. For some time neither spoke. Badger felt that Fox had something on his mind, so he remained quiet until his friend should be ready to talk. He watched the snowflakes settle on Fox's lithe chestnut body, grizzling his fur and making him appear prematurely aged.

At length Fox said, 'If we do have a long spell of snow, I shall have to start making plans for a food supply.'

'I don't think that will be necessary just yet,' Badger said calmly. 'We can see how things develop. The animals will make shift for themselves.'

'Of course they will,' said Fox hurriedly. 'They'll have to. But I have a feeling in my bones about this winter and – well, quite frankly, Badger, I'm more than a little concerned.'

Badger felt he should allay his companion's fears if he could. 'Don't go worrying yourself,' he told him. 'After all, to begin with Toad and Adder and the hedgehogs are not involved. I can look after myself and so can Weasel, Tawny Owl and Kestrel. Of the smaller creatures, the squirrels have only to dig up a fraction of their buried treasure to survive, and Mole has never been so well supplied. So who does that leave? Hare and his family, the rabbits, the voles and the fieldmice. All of *them* eat seeds and vegetation. You're a carnivore. You couldn't begin to be as proficient at finding stores of their food as they are themselves.'

'Yes, I suppose you're right,' Fox agreed. 'It's just that if any of them do get into difficulties I shall feel responsible for getting them out.'

'It's early days yet,' said Badger. 'You just think about Vixen for the time being. The others will manage, you'll see.'

'You're always a comforting chap,' Fox said warmly, 'and I'm truly grateful, Badger.'

They reached the Hollow together and Fox's next words made it clear that Badger had not succeeded in putting his mind at rest.

'This is where our new life began last summer,' he said, looking down at the familiar meeting-place of the Farthing Wood community. 'Let's hope the next few months won't see the end of it for some of us.'

—3—
First Losses

The first signs were not good for wild creatures as the old year drew to a close. December came in with a blizzard, and over the next few weeks a cruel, bitter frost held the Park in its grip night after night. During the daylight hours the sun gleamed fitfully but snow clouds blotted it out for most of the day, and so very little of the frost disappeared. The ground became as hard as iron, and ice coated the Edible Frogs' pond to a thickness of two inches.

A stream ran through most of the Reserve and, some distance from where the Farthing Wood animals had set up home, Whistler the heron could be found. He had chosen an area under some overhanging alder trees where fish abounded in the shallow reaches. Now each day he and his mate watched the slower-moving water by the stream's banks gather more ice. Soon only the centre of the stream, where it rippled swiftly over the tinkling pebbles, continued to flow. Whistler had to step on to the ice to be able to continue his hunting, but the fish were less plentiful further out in the water and the heron and his mate began to notice their diet suffering.

'It looks, my dear, as if we shall have to be rather less choosy in our fare,' Whistler observed in his slow, precise manner. 'From your greater knowledge of the Park, can you suggest any fresh avenues of approach?'

The female heron nodded. 'I told you long ago of a place upstream, where the water runs very fast, and which abounds in crayfish. But you told me you had no liking for shellfish.'

Whistler shrugged his great wings. 'Obviously I shall have to overcome my aversion, at least temporarily. Show me the way, if you please.'

The two water birds rose into the air together, their long, thin legs trailing beneath them like pairs of stilts. From the air, the Park was one vast expanse of rolling white, pierced by clumps of bare, snowclad trees. Whistler's damaged wing shrilled musically with its every beat, and his eyes began to water in the freezing temperature.

They landed after a brief flight, and Whistler's mate began to search the stream-bed. Here the water was completely free of ice. Suddenly her pointed beak stabbed downwards, and then re-emerged firmly clenching a feebly moving crayfish, which she swallowed at a gulp. Whistler joined the hunt and was soon successful. His mate watched for his reaction. 'Hm,' he murmured, swallowing hard. 'Not at all bad. It's surprising how an empty stomach may overcome the most rooted prejudice.'

As there were fish also to be had in this stretch of water, the two birds made an excellent meal. His satisfaction made Whistler call his friends from Farthing Wood to mind. He wondered what difficulties they might be experiencing.

'We mustn't be selfish,' he told his mate. 'This food source might well be of benefit to others. While you return to the roost, my clever one, I think I'll search out Fox and see if I can be of use to him.'

Accordingly he flew off in the direction of Fox's earth. As it was daylight he did not expect to find his friend above ground, and was surprised to see a very lean Vixen sitting by one of the entrance holes when he arrived. She appeared to be very disconsolate, but bravely tried to look cheerful as she greeted the heron.

'Is Fox below?' Whistler asked her.

'No,' she replied. 'Things have been getting rather hard, and he decided to go and see for himself how everyone else is coping.'

'The very reason I came to see you,' Whistler explained, and went on to describe his earlier success in the stream.

Despite her efforts at control, Vixen's mouth began to water freely as she heard of the fish Whistler and his mate had enjoyed.

'It would be more than a pleasure for me to help you catch some,' Whistler offered.

'I'm sure Fox would be most grateful,' Vixen said appreciatively. 'I think I should wait for him to return before we go. There might be one or two other animals who would like to join us.'

'I wonder how long he will be?' Whistler asked.

'I don't know exactly,' answered Vixen, 'but he's already been gone some hours.'

While they waited, she explained how their hunting

trips had become steadily less fruitful and how their diet
had become one of carrion, insects and even snails when
they had discovered a hibernating colony. 'But they
tasted so good,' she added.

'Oh yes,' agreed the heron. 'I myself have made some
adjustments in my eating pattern,' and he went on to
tell her of the crayfish he had eaten.

Presently they saw the familiar figure of Fox ap-
proaching them, accompanied by a smaller one they
could not at first distinguish. It turned out to be Weasel.

Whistler and the two animals greeted each other with
pleasure. But Fox's expression returned to one of deep
concern when Vixen questioned him on his discoveries.

'It's even worse than I'd expected,' he informed her
miserably. 'The voles and fieldmice have already lost a
considerable number of their party, and some of the
older rabbits have died of the severe cold. If this weather
continues for a long spell the mice, in particular, are
going to be decimated.'

Whistler expressed his sympathy but, privately, was
more alarmed at Fox's own appearance. Gone was the
vigorous, supple body of the resourceful leader the
animals had come to rely on during their long trek to
the Nature Reserve. Gone was the bright-eyed, healthful
expression of his face. And gone was the rich lustre of
his coat, that had marked Fox as a creature in his prime.
Now his eyes were downcast, his fur dull and staring,
his movements slow and hesitant, while his body was
not so much lean as distinctly bony. By comparison
Weasel's much smaller form, always as slim as a sapling,
looked in much better shape.

Whistler hurriedly told Fox about the proposed fish-
ing. Without a great deal of interest, Fox agreed. Then
he said, 'But of what use are fish to voles and fieldmice?
They are hungry too.'

'Of course they are,' said Vixen. 'But you must keep your strength up if you wish to help them, even though that is going to be difficult.'

'Rabbits and fieldmice soon replace their numbers,' Whistler pointed out in an attempt to ease Fox's mind.

'Yes, but there may be no stock of fieldmice to replace numbers from,' Fox muttered. 'Their community has lost more in the last week than during the whole of our journey across the countryside. And the voles haven't fared much better.'

'Did you see Hare?' Vixen asked him.

'Yes. His family are all reasonably well though, like everyone else, they've taken on a lean look. The leverets are almost up to his size now, and quite independent.'

'How is Badger?' Whistler wanted to know.

'He wasn't at home,' replied Fox. 'But I've no fears on his account. He has more experience of life than any of us. He'll survive.'

'I'm sure we'll see a thaw soon,' said Weasel optimistically. 'The winter has a long way to go yet, and a cold spell like this rarely lasts for more than a few weeks.'

Fox did not reply, but they all knew he was wondering what could be done if it lasted through to the spring.

Whistler gave them directions to the fishing area and told them he would meet them there. When they arrived, they found he had wasted no time. Four reasonably sized fish and a couple of crayfish awaited them. The three animals fell to at once and made short work of the meal. Whistler enquired if they had had enough.

'Better to save some for another day,' remarked Vixen, 'than to feast now and starve tomorrow.'

Whistler acknowledged her wisdom. Then he said, 'I've seen nothing of the other birds. Has anyone encountered them recently?'

'Oh, Tawny Owl can always be found in his beech

coppice,' Weasel answered. 'He was dozing when we came past just now. He's found himself a snug hollow trunk out of this biting air. As to Kestrel, he flies so far afield you would be lucky to catch a glimpse of him.'

The animals enquired after the health of Whistler's mate. As she was the favourite topic of the heron's conversation, he answered enthusiastically. 'Oh, she is such a wonderful creature,' he told them. 'It was she, of course, who knew where to find the crayfish and showed me the spot. I'm sure I never shall be able to express sufficient gratitude to you all for allowing me to accompany you on your journey to the Park. Had I not met you, I should still be patrolling the waterside in that quarry, with no more company than a lot of raucous mallards and coots. Now I'm living in that perfect contentment of a paired wild creature which I'm sure you, Fox, also enjoy.'

Fox and Vixen smiled at each other and Weasel chuckled. 'Hold on,' he said. 'Some of us still opt for the single state, you know.'

'Ah, not for long, Weasel, if you are a wise beast,' Whistler admonished him. 'There is no comparison, I assure you.'

Weasel laughed again. 'Perhaps you're right,' he said. 'But, on the other hand, "better the devil you know" and so forth.'

This little exchange served to lighten their mood, and provided a welcome relief from their troubles. The animals thanked Whistler heartily for his generosity and, telling him to keep in touch, began to make their way back along the bank of the stream towards their homes. Dusk fell early at that time of year, and the cloud-covered sky hastened the darkness. Weasel left the fox couple for his den, and as Fox and Vixen approached the earth, they could see an agitated Mole waiting for them.

'Whatever is the matter?' Fox asked at once.

'Badger's disappeared,' said the distraught little crea-
ture, and broke into a sob.

'Now, now, calm down, Mole,' Fox said soothingly.
'He always leaves his set at this time in the evening.
You know that.'

'Yes, but he hasn't been in it all day either,' wailed
Mole. 'I've been along my connecting tunnel half a
dozen times today to see him, and the set has been
empty all along.'

Fox looked at Vixen. 'Hm,' he mused. 'That does
seem strange.'

'I'm sure there's some simple explanation for his ab-
sence,' said Vixen. 'He may be on a visit or – '

'He wouldn't be likely to go visiting in this weather,'
interrupted Mole. 'I'm so worried. Badger's habits never
change. He sleeps during the day, and only wakes up in
the evening.'

'When did you last see him?' Fox asked.

'Yesterday. We talked about the shortage of food, and
I offered him some of my worms because he said *I* was
looking plumper than usual. Then he started to talk
about you, Fox, saying that it wasn't fair for you alone
to feel responsible for all the animals' welfare, and that
he was sure you were getting thinner and thinner be-
cause of it, and you needed some help.'

'That's Badger all over, the dear kind creature,' Vixen
observed.

'Yes, and it makes the picture much clearer,'
announced Fox. 'He's obviously gone off on some ven-
ture of his own with the idea of helping us in one way
or another, though Heaven knows what he can possibly
do. Don't be too alarmed, Mole. I think we shall see
him back by the morning, and I'll ask Tawny Owl to
keep an eye open for him tonight.'

'But what if he doesn't return?' persisted Mole. 'I know I shan't be comfortable until I know he's all right.'

'If he doesn't return,' replied Fox, 'I shall personally go out tomorrow to search for him, even if it means combing the entire Park.'

'Oh, thank you, Fox,' said Mole. 'I knew you would. I'll go home and stop bothering you now, and I'll look into Badger's set in the morning and let you know.'

Fox trotted off to speak to Tawny Owl, leaving Vixen and Mole to return to the comparative warmth of their underground shelters.

4
The Search for Badger

Mole went straight to Badger's set before he ate a single worm the next day which, in his case, was the strongest possible measure of his anxiety. The set was, again, empty. He emerged from one of Badger's exit tunnels and made his way as fast as his short legs would allow him to Fox, cursing his slowness as he did so. But his journey proved unnecessary for, when he reached the earth, Vixen informed him that Fox had already set off on his search. He had wasted no time on hearing from Tawny Owl that Badger had not been seen returning home, and all that they could do now was to wait for news.

It was not long before Fox realized that, if he did not find Badger within the area of the Reserve settled by the

Farthing Wood animals, or at least close by, he would
never have the strength to travel the confines of the
whole of White Deer Park. In addition to his own weaker
state, there was the powdery snow, which in places had
formed thick drifts, and was very tiring to walk through
as he frequently sank in it as deep as his shoulders. Even
as he trudged along it again began to snow heavily, so
that visibility became very poor too.

Skirting the Hollow, he made a tour of the perimeter
of their home area. The falling snow covered any tracks
or scent that might have been useful, and Fox knew he
was on an impossible task. He must recruit some assist-
ance. A swifter and less heavy animal such as Hare
would be able to cover a greater distance more easily,
but most of all Fox wished for a sight of Kestrel. His
piercing eyesight from high above the ground could lo-
cate the lumbering form of Badger faster than anyone's.
For the moment, however, he must make do with Hare.

Luckily Hare was to be found sheltering with his mate
in a scooped-out 'form' of snow behind a hawthorn tree.
The leverets were elsewhere. Fox explained why he had
come again so soon.

'That *is* surprising,' Hare said afterwards, 'old Badger
going off like that. I wonder what he intended to do?'

'We've no way of knowing, at the moment,' answered
Fox. 'The thing I'm afraid of is that he might have met
with some accident. He doesn't normally wander far
afield.'

'How can I help?' Hare asked.

'You're much fleeter of foot than me,' replied Fox,
'and can cover greater distances more easily. If I comb
this side of the Park, could you investigate a bit further
afield?'

Hare was silent for a time. Eventually he said cau-
tiously, 'I *could*. But I don't relish the idea of going too

far away from the home area. After all, there are other foxes in the Park beside yourself and Vixen, and I'm fair game for all of them.'

Fox nodded. 'I know,' he said. 'But I've never yet met a fox who could outrun a hare.'

Hare's mate had pricked up her ears at this latter turn in the conversation. 'Don't put his life too much at risk,' she begged Fox. 'He's the father of a family, you know. Badger is a loner and would leave behind no mate to mourn.'

'No, but the number of creatures who would mourn the loss of Badger would be far greater,' Fox pointed out.

Hare looked from one to the other, torn between conflicting loyalties.

'Well, I shan't press you,' Fox said finally. 'It may be that your duty to your family should come first, after all.' He started to move away, but Hare called him back.

'I *will* go,' he announced. 'I should never forgive myself if I turned down such a request for help.'

'Thank you,' said Fox simply. He described where he wanted Hare to go – the area beyond the Edible Frogs' pond. 'We'll confer later at the Hollow,' he added. 'I shall be there at dusk. Good luck.'

He left the two animals but did not fail to hear Hare being up-braided by his mate as he went – 'Why did you let him talk you into it like that?' and Hare's quiet reply, 'For the sake of Farthing Wood.' Now as Fox plodded on through the relentless snowfall, his spirits rose a little and some of the tiredness left him. He found some harder patches of snow, where it had begun to thaw and then frozen over, and he was able to increase his speed, all the time casting about for his old friend.

He came out into the open expanse of parkland where the White Deer herd usually roamed, and it was not long before he spotted a group of them feeding from bales of hay specially provided by the conscientious Warden. One of their number was the Great Stag himself, a huge figure who now did not look so imposing as before. The hard winter was taking its toll of all creatures, from the highest to the lowest. Against the dazzling snow carpet, the white hides of the deer looked duller than Fox had remembered. The Stag noticed him and stepped elegantly towards him.

'How do things go with you and yours?' he asked.

'Not well,' Fox answered. 'Food is hard to come by and the cold very cruel.'

'Yes, I don't recall many winters such as this,' said the Stag. 'For some reason this year *we* are not to be expected to fend entirely for ourselves. The humans, in their wisdom, have decided to buffer us against extreme hardship.'

'I understand your herd is unique,' said Fox, 'so it isn't surprising that your numbers are not allowed to become too depleted.'

The Stag nodded sagely. 'I'm only sorry you don't eat hay,' he said. 'We have more than enough.'

Fox thought of the rabbits and mice. 'There is something you could do,' he said, 'if you are so willing. My smaller, weaker friends are suffering particularly. If you didn't object, perhaps some stray stalks could be left aside for their use?'

'Of course. Certainly,' the Great Stag agreed readily. 'But you don't often come to these parts, do you? It would be a really difficult undertaking for creatures smaller than yourself.'

'That's true,' Fox answered. 'But if they are sufficiently hungry I'm sure they will come.'

The Great Stag pondered a moment. 'It is most unusual,' he observed, 'this mutual co-operation and concern your band of animals feels for each other. Normally, in the wild, each animal goes his own way and – well, the strongest survive. I find the idea of helping one another most interesting – even appealing. Perhaps we deer should also show a willingness to assist our brother creatures. Supposing I arrange it that each member of my herd carries a mouthful of hay and deposits it at a point more conveniently close to your friends?'

'That would indeed be kind,' Fox told him, and added that the best place to leave the food would be by the Hollow.

'It shall be done today,' the Stag said. 'But tell me, my friend, what brought you this way in the first place?'

'One of our party – Badger – has disappeared,' said Fox. 'I'm looking for him.'

'Hm, again this concern for others. Most interesting,' intoned the doyen of the deer herd. 'Well, if I hear of his whereabouts I shall most certainly come and tell you. I wish you all well.' He rejoined the rest of the herd and Fox continued on his way.

Presently he came within sight of the Warden's cottage and garden area beyond the fence and here he struck lucky again, for Kestrel was perched on top of one of the palings. The hawk called joyfully to him and flew over, wheeling playfully over Fox's head.

'Come down, Kestrel, I want your help,' shouted Fox.

The bird was at once all seriousness, and landed beside him. 'What is it?' he asked.

Fox told him.

'I'll go now – at once. Earlier today I was flying over the Park, but I had no sign of Badger.'

Fox told him of the rendezvous at dusk in the Hollow with Hare; then he said, 'Before you go, can I ask you to stay closer at hand for the next few days? You might be needed again.'

Kestrel agreed and swooped off to begin his exploration.

For the rest of the day, Fox methodically combed every part of the Reserve he could before he felt exhaustion to be imminent. With the last reserves of his strength he made his slow way back towards the meeting point. The snow had ceased by the time he reached the Hollow, where he discovered Vixen, Mole, Weasel and Tawny Owl waiting for news. He merely shook his head as he saw them.

Mole said nothing, almost as if he dare not speak.

'I asked Hare and Kestrel to help me,' Fox said wearily. 'I'm more hopeful of their news.'

Hare was the next to arrive, but he had no comfort for them. However they tried not to feel too disheartened until Kestrel had come.

'If anyone can find Badger that hawk can do it,' Weasel said encouragingly.

'Unfortunately that remark implies,' Tawny Owl pointed out, 'that if Kestrel can't find him the rest of us don't have a chance.'

They fell silent again, shifting their feet in the bitter cold. At last Kestrel arrived.

'I've searched every corner of the Reserve twice over,' he told them, 'and found not a trace of Badger anywhere. He seems to have disappeared into thin air.'

Mole broke down at this appalling news of his beloved Badger, and it was left to Vixen to try and console him.

'He can't just have vanished,' muttered Fox. 'There's something very odd about this.'

'Perhaps he's been adopted into another set?' suggested Hare.

'Never – not our Badger,' declared Weasel.

'Unless he were coerced?' Tawny Owl added.

'This is what is worrying me,' Fox admitted. 'It seems

the only solution: that Badger has somehow managed to get himself captured and taken underground, or at any rate carried off by something. But no, no . . . it's incredible.'

'Well, there's nothing any of us can do for the moment,' remarked Tawny Owl. 'I'm famished, and I need longer than usual to hunt up my supper these days. I'll bid you farewell till tomorrow.'

He had not been long gone, when the animals espied a group of deer coming towards them. Fox told of his talk with the Great White Stag, and they all watched as each deer dropped its mouthful of hay by the Hollow and quietly retreated. This put other thoughts into Fox's mind.

'Hare, on your way home, will you inform your cousins the rabbits about this?'

'I'll have a mouthful or two myself first,' he answered.

'I'll go and tell those poor mice,' Fox continued.

'No,' said Weasel. 'You're far too tired. You go and rest. *I'll* tell them.'

Fox was about to relate the Great Stag's comments on their mutual help for each other, but he was simply too worn out, and allowed Vixen to lead him back to their den.

Mole was the last to leave the Hollow. 'I won't believe it,' he kept muttering to himself. 'He *hasn't* disappeared. I'll find him. I'll find him.'

5
What had Happened to Badger

Badger had thought long and hard about the animals'
difficulties, and it had occurred to him that none of them
had any idea how the original inhabitants of the Reserve
were coping with the winter. As they would know the
resources of the Park far better than the recent arrivals
from Farthing Wood, he decided there would be no harm
done if he went to seek out advice where he could.

Saying nothing to any of his friends, he left his home
at his usual time in the evening and set off on his quest.
The night air was still and the moon glowed from a clear
sky. It was intensely cold and Badger hurried along as
quickly as he could with his rather shambling gait.

He had left the familiar region of the Park far behind before he encountered another creature. Under some shrubbery he surprised a stoat who was feeding from the carcase of a rabbit. The two strangers eyed each other warily.

'It's a bitter night,' Badger said at length.

'There's not enough for two,' the stoat replied, who obviously thought he had a competitor for his meal.

'I'm not after your food,' Badger told him. 'I can see you are very hungry.'

'Famished,' answered the stoat bluntly. 'Haven't eaten for three days.'

'Hunting difficult?' Badger asked unnecessarily.

'That's an understatement,' came the reply. 'There's nothing about. This rabbit died from the cold, I should say. Of course, it's frozen solid. But you have to eat what you can these days.' The animal wrenched off another mouthful and appeared to find it of great relish. 'What about you?' the stoat enquired. 'I don't think I've seen you around before.'

'No, you wouldn't have,' Badger told him. 'I don't usually wander as far as this. I'm one of the newcomers to the Park.'

'Oh, you're one of the great travellers, are you?' the stoat said with a touch of cynicism. 'Well, you've found no garden of abundance here, I'll bet.'

'Who could have expected weather like this?' Badger answered. 'In any case, the whole countryside must be affected.'

'Of course,' agreed the stoat. 'This winter will halve the population of this Reserve, though.'

'Do you think so? As bad as that?'

'Bound to,' the animal said shortly. 'Very little food means very few survive.'

Badger nodded. 'Yes, I suppose so.'

The stoat seemed to be waiting to be left alone again. Badger eventually noticed. 'Er – I'm sorry to have interrupted you,' he said. 'I'll leave you in peace.' He moved away and called back a hesitant, 'Good luck!' over his shoulder, but the stoat was too busy with his meal to respond.

However, the remarks he had made to Badger had made it pretty evident that none of the creatures in the Park was faring very well. He thought of the Great Stag, whose wisdom could perhaps serve the animals' interests in their hardship. But where was he to be found? Not in the woods, at any rate. He would be in open country. Badger continued on his way.

But he never reached the deer herd, though they were in his sights before the accident happened. He was descending a slight slope which was very slippery with ice. His feet skidded and he went hurtling down, unable to stop himself, just like a toboggan. At the bottom of the slope was a large rock. Badger was completely powerless to avoid it. One side of his body and one hind leg struck the rock heavily. Badly winded, he let out a cry of pain at the blow on his leg. When he could breathe freely again, he tried to hoist himself upright, but such a searing agony shot through the injured hind leg that he merely collapsed on his side once more.

There he lay for the rest of the night. He knew there was no possibility of walking, and the dreadful cold seemed to penetrate every inch of his fur. He wondered what would ever become of him. 'What hope have I got?' he asked himself. 'I'm a long way from my friends, I've no food, no shelter, and I can't move.' He fell into an uneasy doze.

When morning came, Badger awoke so cold and stiff he could barely even raise his head. But salvation was on the way, although he did not know it. The Warden

of the Park had been out distributing the bales of hay
for the White Deer herd, and was doing a general round
of the Reserve in his Land Rover. Stopping periodically
to view an area through his field-glasses, he spotted the
almost inert form of Badger and went to investigate. In
no time Badger found himself being lifted, taken to the
vehicle where he was laid gently down amongst some
old rugs, and transported back to the warmth and com-
fort of the Warden's cottage kitchen.

The Warden fetched an old dog basket, lined it with
sacking and old cloths and deposited the uncomplaining
Badger inside. Then he stood contemplating the animal
thoughtfully for a minute, before beginning to prepare
some food. Badger fell into another doze, induced by his
weakness and the warmth of the room.

When he next sleepily raised his eyelids, he found
some raw mince and warm milk placed in front of him.
He was able to move his body sufficiently to feed and he
ate greedily. His rescuer appeared to be delighted with
this, for Badger sensed eyes on him and looked up. The
man was smiling broadly, and Badger was astonished,
almost numbed by the brightness of the human face.
Never had he been so close to humankind before. There
was something mysterious – awe-inspiring – there: some-
thing quite beyond his own experience and
understanding.

But the Warden did not linger. Badger was left to
finish his meal and rest in peace. As he sank back on
the bed provided for him, he thought of his friends in
the Park that he had wanted to help. A lot of help *he*
had been to them. They were still suffering in the bleak
winter weather – battling against elements that soon
could overwhelm them entirely. He knew that his
absence would be noticed. The animals would be ignor-
ant of his fate, and he as ignorant of theirs. Would he

be able to walk again? He realized the Warden wished
to aid his recovery. But how long would he be kept here?
He despised feeling so helpless.

Eventually his very helplessness overcame him, and
in his weak state he fell asleep again. He did not know
that, on several occasions while he slept, the Warden
looked in, and was amused by his snoring. But there
was a fresh supply of mince and water to drink when he
woke at his usual hour in the evening.

When he had finished eating again, he became aware
of a presence in the room, although he had heard nothing
moving. In the gloom that he was so used to he soon
noticed a pair of green eyes watching him unblinkingly
from the doorway. They belonged to a large ginger cat,
the Warden's pet.

'You're in a bad way,' the animal remarked, and
walked on noiseless feet towards him in an elaborately
unhurried way. By the basket the cat bent and sniffed
curiously at Badger for a long time. 'You have the rank
smell of a wild creature,' he announced.

The creature's coolness nonplussed Badger. He was
not a mouse or a pigeon, but a large untamed animal
whose normal strength must be totally unknown to the
cat.

'Have you been eating my meat?' was the next
question.

'Your master fed me,' Badger replied.

'I have no master,' the cat responded at once. 'I am
my own master. I do as I choose.'

'Then why do you choose to eat meat provided by a
human?' Badger asked subtly.

'Why ever not?' the cat wanted to know, flicking his
tail slightly in irritation. 'It saves me the trouble of
finding it for myself.'

Badger was silent.

'I've no objection to your eating it, anyway,' the cat said nonchalantly. 'There's plenty more where that came from, and all sorts of other things as well. Do you like fish?'

'I've eaten fish on occasion, yes,' Badger answered.

'Hm. What do you usually eat?'

'Grubs, roots, bulbs, small creatures. . . .'

'Rats?'

'Sometimes.'

'Good. Then we have something in common. My chief pleasure is hunting rats.'

'Are there many around here?' Badger asked, immediately thinking of their value to Fox and Vixen and Tawny Owl, too.

'Not since I arrived on the scene,' replied the cat boastfully, flexing his claws. 'The man brought me here as a kitten two winters ago.'

Their conversation was cut short by the sound of human steps. The Warden came into the room, and Badger was astounded to see a complete change of character come over the domestic animal. Running to its owner, it became at once the playful and affectionate pet, rubbing itself round his legs and purring noisily; then scampering off to a corner before returning to repeat the performance. The man spoke to his pet which increased the volume of purring instantly.

Badger soon understood it was the cat's mealtime now and the leg-rubbing ritual, together with stretching and mewing, continued until the food was ready. It then abruptly stopped while the more important task of eating was taken care of.

Badger came in for a word or two from the Warden also, though of course he understood nothing. Yet the sounds were very pleasing to him and comforting, too, and he was quite sure that had been the intention.

When the Warden left the kitchen again, the cat followed him. A short time afterwards he returned to put his ginger head round the door. 'I'm going to spend the rest of the evening in front of the fire,' he informed Badger. 'I feel very sleepy. But we'll talk again later. I hope you're comfortable for now?'

Badger assured him he was, and found himself alone again. He was soon musing over the strange mixture of his new acquaintance's personality: semi-domesticated and yet semi-independent. Despite himself, he felt drawn to the animal. He promised to be an interesting source of information.

Outside it was snowing again. In the warmth and security of the basket, Badger felt distinctly guilty as he thought again of his old companions. How he wished they could be sharing his new-found comfort with him now.

—6—
Conversations

The next day Badger felt a good deal stronger after plenty of rest and food. He particularly enjoyed a couple of apples the Warden thoughtfully gave him. With his returning strength, he began to look forward to being active again, and was pleased to receive another visit from the cat as a relief from the monotony.

The cat came running into the kitchen, his ginger fur glistening where the snowflakes were melting. 'It's really quite dreadfully cold out there,' he announced. 'Far too cold for me. I bet you'd sooner be in here too.'

'It's certainly warm here,' Badger admitted. 'But my set was always quite cosy, you know. There was plenty of dried bracken and leaves and grass and so on to pull round oneself.'

'But didn't the snow cover you?' asked the cat.

'No, no, my home's underground,' Badger explained.

The cat looked surprised. 'Underground? How extraordinary,' he said.

'Not extraordinary at all,' Badger said a little defensively. 'A lot of wild creatures live underground. It's a lot safer and, as I said, very comfortable.'

'Who are your enemies?' whispered the cat.

'Humans principally,' Badger replied. 'And dogs.'

'Well, you've no fear from humans hereabouts,' the cat reassured him in a well-meaning way. 'There aren't any, except the man here, and he loves all wild creatures.'

'I know there's nothing to fear here,' Badger replied. 'That's why we all came to the Reserve in the first place. For safety.'

'Where did you come from, then?'

'Oh, a long, long way away. A place called Farthing Wood. We had to leave, because the humans were destroying the wood. Our homes were threatened, and if we had stayed we would have been killed.'

'How many other badgers were with you?' asked the cat.

'None. We were a motley party. Fox, Weasel, Tawny Owl, Mole, Toad, Kestrel, along with hedgehogs and rabbits and hares and squirrels and voles and fieldmice and even a snake.'

'This is most interesting,' declared the cat. 'It sounds as if half the countryside was on the march.'

'It wasn't really like that,' Badger smiled. 'We were only a small band and, naturally, we lost some of our number on the way. Considering the hazards we encountered, we were fortunate not to lose more.'

'I see,' said the cat, who did not at all. 'The mice were taken to provide food for you on the way.'

'No, no, no,' Badger cried in horror. 'They were companions on our journey. Before we set out, we all swore an oath to protect each other's safety – not to molest one another.'

'But surely,' persisted the cat, 'in the wild it is common for stronger animals to prey on the weak?'

Badger nodded. 'But we are no common group of animals,' he said with the greatest satisfaction.

'I'm beginning to understand that,' remarked the cat. 'Tell me about your adventures.'

'With pleasure,' said Badger. 'And the only way to do that is to begin at the beginning.'

So the cat sat perfectly still while he heard about the animals' escape from Farthing Wood and their journey across country, with all the dangers they had faced of the fire, the river crossing, the Hunt and the motorway. He also heard how the animals had seen the Warden before arriving at the Park. 'Well, well,' he said afterwards, 'quite a story. Makes my life seem very dull.'

'Each to his own,' Badger said sagely. 'I imagine you're content with your lot?'

'Oh yes, I have everything I want. Food, warmth – and I can come and go as I please. A cat can be happy with very little.'

'Have you never felt the desire to be completely free, completely in charge of your own life?' Badger enquired.

'But I am,' the cat protested. 'As I told you, I please myself.'

'It's not what we wild creatures would call really free,' Badger said provokingly. 'I rather think you're more attached to the man than you care to admit. I was interested to see the way you responded to him yesterday – you made quite a fuss of him.'

'Oh well,' the cat answered, beginning to lick his chest fur as a diversion, 'they expect something for their pains, don't they? The man likes to think I'm dependent on him.'

'Perhaps you are?'

'Not at all,' the cat said huffily. 'I can survive perfectly well on my own if I have to. You're just trying to rile me.'

'I certainly am not,' Badger said at once. 'But I'll tell you what. Once I can walk again I shall leave here. Why don't you come with me and prove to the human you don't really need him?'

The cat did not take up the challenge. 'How *is* your leg?' he asked. 'Still painful?'

Badger indicated that it was. The cat began to lick the wound sympathetically. But Badger had to call out to him to stop. 'Your tongue is so rough,' he explained. 'But you're very kind.'

There were human voices outside. The cat jumped up to the window-sill to look. 'Ah,' he said. 'The man who makes animals well is coming. He often comes here when a wild creature has been found in trouble. He will help you.'

The Warden came in with another human who was, indeed, a vet. Badger found himself quite unalarmed at being closely examined and tested, and then having his bad leg bound tightly with some materials. The two men then talked for a period, and the Warden seemed to be quite satisfied with what he was told. The vet made a fuss of the cat, calling him by his name, 'Ginger', and tickling his chin. Badger's new friend responded in the way expected, by purring very loudly and nuzzling the proffered finger. Then the animals were left alone again. Badger was amused, and decided to persist with his suggestion of the cat's adopting the wild way of life.

'Well, perhaps I may,' the cat said evasively, 'but I

think it will be quite a while yet before you're fit enough for the man to release you.'

'Release me?' said Badger sharply. 'I'm not to be kept here, am I?'

'Oh no,' said the cat. 'As soon as you are considered to be quite well enough to return to the wild, you'll be taken outside to run away freely.'

'I shouldn't have doubted really,' said Badger. 'I know that man really wants the best for wild creatures. If only all humans were of his type, there would be no need for any beast or bird to fear them. But I believe they are few and far between.'

'Oh, there's not many like him,' the cat averred. 'He's about the best you can hope for from their race.'

Badger noted the enthusiasm in the cat's voice, which certainly did suggest there was a bond of attachment between him and the Warden, despite the animal's claim to be independent. Then he thought of his own attachments. He wished he knew how his old friends were. By now they were sure to be concerned about his disappearance. He dared not think too much about how Mole might be feeling. He watched the cat washing himself meticulously, preparatory to curling up in his own bed. A thought struck him. He himself was unable to go to them, but he could send a messenger. The cat could be his legs.

'I wonder if I could ask you to do me quite a large favour?' Badger asked rather nervously, for he suspected the cat's reaction.

The cat paused in the middle of his toilet, the tip of his tongue protruding from his mouth and one hind leg raised into the air from his squatting position.

'I'm getting increasingly worried about my friends in the Reserve. They don't know where I am,' Badger went on. 'I know they'll be out looking for me, and they've more than enough to cope with just staying alive at the moment, without bothering about me.'

'I think I know what the request is to be,' the cat remarked, lying down.

'*Would* you be able to be so obliging as to carry a message of my safety to them?'

'To be perfectly honest,' the cat said, 'I don't think it is possible. Your friends are meat-eaters, or some of them are. They don't know me, and they're very hungry. Don't you think I would be exposing myself to more than a reasonable risk of attack by a fox or an owl?'

'I'm sure you would be too large a morsel for an owl,' Badger said reassuringly. 'As for Fox and Vixen they, like Tawny Owl, are mostly inactive in the daytime. You would be quite safe then, even if they might pose a threat after dark, which I personally don't believe. You are a reasonably large animal yourself, and sure to be beyond their scope. In any case, you showed no fear of *me* from the outset.'

'But I knew you were sick,' the cat pointed out, 'otherwise you wouldn't have been here. And, even if I am safe in daytime, I don't know the terrain. The Park is enormous, and completely covered by snow. I'd sink up to my neck at the first step.'

'No, you're too light-footed for that. You've been outside the cottage, anyway, in the snow.'

'Yes, but most of it has been cleared by the man where *we* want to walk. If I went into the depths of the Park where would I shelter? It would be a long trek to where your friends live, and then to come back again.'

'You could shelter in my set and be quite warm and safe,' Badger offered unrealistically. 'Any of them would show you where it is.'

'Impossible,' the cat declared roundly. 'I couldn't go

underground. No, I'm sorry, my friend, because I would like to help. But I really don't see that I can.'

Badger resorted to a final means of persuasion. Affecting a slightly malicious tone he said, 'So I was right. You couldn't survive alone, without human assistance.'

The cat looked at him angrily for a second. 'You seem to forget I wasn't born in the wild like you and your friends,' he snapped. 'I haven't the long experience of the lore of survival you have acquired from birth. You tell me you wild creatures are literally battling for life in what are, after all, exceptionally bad conditions. How well do you think I will manage, without the knowledge you are armed with?'

Badger felt this was an honest enough answer and that it would not be seemly to pursue the argument. But his friends *must* be informed. 'Then there's no alternative,' he told the cat quietly. 'I accept what you say as reasonable, and so it means I shall have to go myself.'

'Don't be so ridiculous!' cried the cat impatiently. 'I can understand you are fond of your friends, but you are taking unselfishness too far. They will just have to get along without you for a bit. You *can't* walk now, but it shouldn't be too long before you are able to return to them – perhaps a couple of weeks. I don't know how serious the damage is. Who knows? Perhaps the worst of the winter will be over by then.'

Badger shook his head. 'I couldn't possibly leave them in ignorance for a matter of weeks,' he persisted doggedly. 'You don't seem to understand. That oath we swore back in Farthing Wood – it hasn't lapsed. My friends won't just accept that I've vanished away. They will be risking their necks to find me.'

'Humph!' the cat snorted irritably. 'You seem to have a very high opinion of yourself.'

'Don't be absurd,' retorted Badger. 'Oh, you can say

what you like, but I've got to get word to them. If you won't go I mean what I say. I shall go myself even if it means crawling all the way.'

The cat realized he was in a corner. He could not possibly allow the crippled Badger to throw his life away, for that was what it would mean. So he had to relent.

'Very well, you've convinced me,' he said with reluctance. 'I'll start tomorrow if it isn't snowing. You'd better describe your friends to me in detail, so that I can recognize them.'

'I shall never forget this, Ginger Cat,' Badger said warmly. 'And, believe me, neither will the other animals. You've just made yourself a host of new friends.'

'Well, Badger' – the cat smiled – 'you're a very persuasive fellow.'

'You are now party to the Oath that binds all the creatures of Farthing Wood, Vixen and Whistler,' Badger reminded him. 'That means, if ever you yourself are in danger or difficulties – well, I think you understand me?'

'We understand each other,' said Ginger Cat.

7

A Meeting

No snow was falling in the morning and two very different animals, who were destined to meet that very day, were preparing to set out from opposite ends of the Park on behalf of Badger.

From the Warden's cottage Ginger Cat, having bade farewell to his new friend, was emerging. He jumped over the fence and looked with foreboding at the great white expanse before him over which he would have to travel. His first faltering steps found the snow surface reasonably firm, and his courage rose slightly. But he knew it was a long way in difficult conditions to Badger's companions.

Meanwhile in Badger's own set, Mole had determined to begin his search. He had formed the idea that Badger had somehow got lost or injured underground as he was not to be seen anywhere on the surface. So he had decided that, as he, Mole, was quite the kingpin among subterranean travellers, it should be he who must search this new area. He began by investigating all of Badger's tunnels in case he had had an accident while digging close to home. Of course he found no sign of any mishap. His next task was to surface and look for any other holes in the neighbourhood where Badger might have entered. This labour of love was as doomed to failure as it was devoted. But Mole kept trying, his stout little heart allowing him to emerge undismayed at every fresh disappointment. Each time he plunged down into the barren, frozen ground he thought that perhaps this time he was going to rescue his poor friend, and it was this idea which made his persevere.

Ginger Cat continued on his way, his silent footsteps taking him slowly, but steadily, towards his goal. He was beginning to feel very chilled and longed for the bright fireside of the cottage, where he basked content in the company of his human companion. As the morning wore on he got colder and colder and regretted his foolhardy mission. After all, what was an injured badger to him? For all the fine words about this wonderful Oath of theirs, he was an outsider, an individual. He was no member of a party. Why should he concern himself with whether Fox or Mole or Weasel or any of the rest of Badger's precious friends should lose their lives looking for him? They were all total strangers to Ginger Cat. Whatever he might have boasted to Badger, he was not a wild creature like they were, having to make shift through the seasons as best they could, come sun, wind, rain, snow and ice. He had an alternative – the alternative of keeping warm and comfortable all day if he felt like it; of sleeping by a blazing fire with a full stomach, ignorant of the raging elements of Nature. It had been his pride alone that had sent him on this absurd journey. Oh, how cold he felt!

All the time the cat was cursing his own misfortune, he was nearing Badger's home area. He passed by the Hollow without knowing its significance and then, suddenly, his senses were alert again as at last he saw movement ahead. He increased his speed and found a small black animal with a long snout crawling out of a hole. It was, of course, Mole.

Mole saw a large unknown animal approaching him and instantly ducked back underground.

'Don't go!' called Ginger Cat down the hole. 'You may be who I'm looking for. I have news of Badger.'

Mole reappeared at once. 'Badger? Where is he? Is he all right? Who are you?'

'He was injured,' Ginger Cat said. 'He's been rescued by the human you call the Naturalist, who is caring for him. Don't worry, he will soon be well.'

Mole did a little jig. 'Thank heaven he's still alive,' he said joyfully. 'But tell me who you are?'

Ginger Cat explained. Then, 'You must be Mole?' he enquired. 'Badger told me you lived underground.'

Mole confessed. 'We've all been so worried,' he said. 'No sign of him for three days. But you are our good friend. You've been very brave.'

'Badger told me about your long journey here from your old home,' said Ginger Cat.

'Will you come and meet the others?' Mole said enthusiastically. 'They'll be so grateful for your news.'

'No, I'm afraid I must decline. I want to be back before it gets dark, and it's a long way.'

'Of course. Tell me, when does Badger think he can come back to us?'

'Oh, Badger would come now if he could,' Ginger Cat

said with a smile. 'But he would be very wise, in my opinion, if he waits for the man to decide. Then he will be sure to be fully well again.'

Mole noticed this tribute to humankind, and realized the cat stood in a different relationship. 'Tell him we are all well,' Mole said. 'At least, tell him we are managing, and that we are missing him terribly.'

'I will, certainly. I hope I may see you again some time,' said Ginger Cat politely.

'Thank you again from all of Farthing Wood,' Mole answered importantly. 'There will always be a greeting for you here.'

Ginger Cat turned to make his way back. Mole watched him go. As the representative of the Farthing Wood community, he wondered if he had handled the meeting correctly. With a start, he remembered he had not offered the cat any refreshment. The animal had made a long journey, and now had the same distance to retrace. There were an abundance of worms in his larder. He called out.

The cat heard the noise and looked round. He could not make out Mole's words for he was a small creature and did not have a strong voice. Mole called again, but Ginger Cat still failed to understand and started to run back.

At that moment Kestrel, who had been patrolling the Park all day from the air for signs of Badger, spotted the two animals on the ground. He saw a large cat running towards his friend Mole, and naturally assumed it was an attack. Wheeling quickly, he dived earthwards and struck Ginger Cat like an arrow, his talons digging deep into the creature's flesh.

The cat howled and lashed out at the bird, but Kestrel was already ascending again for another plunge.

'Stop, Kestrel, stop!' called Mole frantically. 'He's a

friend!' But the hawk was too high to hear and was preparing to launch another strike. 'Quickly, into the hole,' Mole said desperately as the cat was instinctively flattening its body against the ground. Ginger Cat heard, but it was too late to move. Down swooped Kestrel again and Mole hurled himself against the ginger body, so that the hawk hesitated and lost the impetus of the descent. This time he heard Mole's pleas, 'No, no! Keep away, Kestrel! He's a friend – a friend!'

Kestrel landed and looked at Mole questioningly with his piercing eyes. Ginger Cat arched his wounded back and hissed aggressively.

'He came with news of Badger,' Mole explained lamely. 'All the way from the Naturalist's house. He wasn't pouncing on me.' He described the news the cat had brought.

Kestrel apologised inadequately for his actions, and told Mole what he had surmised from the air. He and Mole looked at Ginger Cat's back. The blood was flowing freely from the two large lacerations, dyeing the ginger fur and making it sticky.

'You and your confounded Oath,' muttered Ginger Cat weakly.

'We can't stay here,' said Mole. 'Kestrel, will you fetch Fox? I don't know what to do.'

Fox was not long in arriving on the scene, accompanied by Vixen. Without much difficulty, they persuaded Ginger Cat to go to shelter in their earth. He was too feeble now to argue. As they made their way along, Mole acquainted Fox with Badger's plight and of the cat's journey to see them.

'What a reward for such a good deed,' said Fox bitterly.

'I acted with the best intentions,' Kestrel hastened to

assure them. 'I thought only of Mole. How could I have known?'

'No-one's blaming you,' Fox replied. 'It's just a very unfortunate incident.'

Once inside the earth, Vixen took it upon herself to lick the wounds on the cat's back and to clean his fur. 'They are nasty cuts,' she observed, 'but they aren't bleeding any more. I hope you will share our meal later? When it is dark Fox and I will go out to see what we can find.'

Ginger Cat expressed his thanks and, himself convinced that his feebleness was more due to excessive tiredness than his wounds, fell gratefully asleep.

Mole stayed with him when the foxes went off on their foray and, before they returned, Ginger Cat awoke with a start in even pitcher blackness than before. 'It's all right,' said Mole. 'You're not alone.' The cat was amused at his tiny companion's effort at reassurance. He could have killed Mole with one paw, but of course had no desire to do so.

'You needn't stay, Mole,' he said smoothly. 'I'm a lot better for that nap. I'll be quite happy to wait on my own for my promised supper.'

'Just as you like,' said Mole readily. 'I'm as hungry as can be myself. I think I'll pay a visit to my own food store.' They exchanged farewells and Mole departed.

As soon as Ginger Cat was sure Mole had got right away, he himself stood up, stretched carefully, and shook his coat daintily. Despite himself, he winced at the pain that throbbed in his back. But he was ready to leave. He had no intention of waiting for Fox and Vixen to return. He would go hungry, but at least before morning he would be back in the warmth and cosiness of the cottage.

He emerged into the starlight, shivering in the bitter

cold, but was thankful to see no further snow had fallen.
So his mission had been accomplished and he was gra-
tified to have met Mole, Fox and Vixen. But he cherished
a hope for revenge on the other of Badger's friends he
had encountered. Was he, a cat, to allow himself to be
bested by a bird – his natural prey? Hawk or no hawk,
should the opportunity ever arise Kestrel would find he
had made an error of judgement if he believed he could
inflict any harm on an equally cunning hunter without
redress.

——8——

Recovery

It was almost dawn when Ginger Cat limped back through his special flap into the Warden's lodge. Never before in his life had he felt so weary. He knew Badger would be agog for his news, but he was too tired to face his questions. So he lay down on the hall carpet where he was and dropped into an immediate sleep.

It was the noise of the Warden's rising that woke him. He stood up stiffly to greet the man's arrival. The Warden, of course, was overjoyed to see him but very concerned to find the wounds inflicted by Kestrel. These were attended to in no time and a large saucer of warm milk proffered while a well-deserved meal was prepared.

Badger could barely restrain his impatience for the man to leave the kitchen, but as soon as he did he started eagerly to demand to know all that had happened.

'I met your friends Mole and Fox and Vixen,' said Ginger Cat. 'They were relieved to hear of your safety. I also met Kestrel who is responsible for this,' he added in a hard voice, indicating his newly-bandaged back, and he went on to describe the incident.

'Oh dear, I really am so sorry,' Badger was most contrite. 'I can see exactly how it happened. He won't be able to forgive himself for injuring you.'

'Really?' hissed the cat sarcastically. 'I think he recovered his presence of mind fairly swiftly. It may be news to you that there is no love lost between cats and birds.'

'But I hope you won't hold this mistake against Kestrel,' Badger said worriedly.

Ginger Cat did not reply. Badger looked hard at him, but his bland expression was totally inscrutable.

'I will tell you one thing,' said the cat. 'You have lost your battle to persuade me to live wild. At the risk of appearing soft – and I don't care a jot – I would never leave this comfortable life to join you out there. I have had my taste now. I've experienced the worst weather I've known. I've been into one of your underground homes and pronounce it to be the most cheerless place I've ever seen or, rather, felt. I've seen the reality of what lack of food and poor shelter can do to an animal, and for that I had to look no further than the skinny, underfed bodies of your fox friends. But I'm going to turn the tables on you now. I say to you, Badger, that if you give up your cosy new home here to return to those appalling conditions amongst your friends you are absolutely mad.'

'But this isn't a home,' Badger pointed out. 'I'm merely being tended while I'm hurt. Once I'm on my feet again, whether I wish it or not, I shall be removed to the Park.'

Ginger Cat shrugged. 'You've seen how I behave and remarked on it,' he said. 'I'm quite sure a little feigned affection from you for your human benefactor would be very well received. That seems to be the only reward he expects for doing almost everything for us.'

'No, no,' Badger shook his head, smiling. 'I haven't the necessary technique. It's inbred in you cats to make yourself ingratiating. It's natural to you.'

'Well, I'm sure it wasn't always so,' Ginger Cat responded. 'It must have begun for a definite purpose. Why don't you decide to become the first domesticated badger?'

'No, it wouldn't be appropriate,' Badger replied. 'I'm too old to change my ways now. And, besides, I'm used to living underground, and tunnelling, and sleeping on beds of leaves and grass and moss and so on – not curled up in a basket like a lap dog.'

'Well, at least stay until the warmer weather,' Ginger Cat wheedled. He had become genuinely fond of Badger and was sincere in wishing him to be comfortable.

'Well, well,' nodded Badger, 'we'll see. But I hope you won't forget all about me if I do go. For my part, I can never repay your kindness in making that journey. And then you come back hurt! It's most distressing.'

'You may rest assured I should keep in touch,' declared Ginger Cat. 'But, tell me, is your home any better appointed than Fox's?'

'Oh yes,' Badger laughed. 'He and Vixen live very simply. But you went underground! I'm most impressed.' He chuckled as he thought of it.

Ginger Cat almost laughed. 'It's a topsy-turvy world,' he said. 'We'll have you curled up in front of the fire next.'

The days passed and Badger's leg grew stronger. He was able to limp a little way around the kitchen to begin with, and then the cat introduced him to the main room of the cottage and he practised walking backwards and forwards from one room to the other. After about a fortnight in the Warden's home Badger had become quite accustomed to his new life. Well-fed and well cared for, he looked sleeker and fitter than at any time since leaving Farthing Wood. He looked a new animal, and he began to dread the appearance of his longsuffering friends when he should return to them. He knew they would look haggard by comparison, and he felt they might look at him accusingly, envying his new-found health.

But he had to acknowledge that that was not all he was dubious about. There had been an element of truth in Ginger Cat's words. Perhaps he *had* grown too used to comfort now. He certainly did not relish the prospect of scraping a living again in the freezing desolation of the Park. He was worse equipped to do so now than before his accident. To adjust now to searching once more for his food, to learn again to live on less than he needed to eat and to adapt to those wicked temperatures from which there was no relief, was indeed a daunting thought.

He felt sure that the Warden would not simply turf him out into the cold once he was walking normally again, if there were still no sign of improvement in the weather. The change would be too sudden. So the temptation to stay on where he was, was constantly with him. Yet he knew he would feel guilty if he did stay unnecessarily long. How could he rest content in such luxury while all the time his old companions continued to suffer the worst sort of discomfort? But what if they were to join *him*? Was it possible?

Day after day the same thoughts went through his mind until the time finally arrived when he knew that his injured leg was completely well again. The strapping and bandages had been removed a week before, at the same time as those on Ginger Cat's back. Now he could shuffle around quite normally once more at his old pace. Now he must decide what he should do.

When he next saw Ginger Cat he told him he was completely recovered. The cat looked at him long and straight. 'Well?' he asked at length. 'What are your plans?'

Badger mentioned his idea of his friends joining them under the care of the Warden. 'Would the man take them in? Would he be able to, would he want to?' he kept asking.

'I don't know,' replied Ginger Cat. 'I don't know if he would have room for all. I *am* sure he would do his best for the animals who seemed most in need of help. But will they wish to come here?'

'Now it's my turn to say I don't know,' Badger confessed. 'But I could try persuading them.'

'You would have to exclude the birds,' Ginger Cat said pointedly.

Badger knew what was in his mind. 'I had already ruled them out,' he agreed.

'When will you leave?' the cat asked next.

'As soon as the man lets me go.'

'That will be when you make it apparent you are eager to return to the Park. You'd better make it obvious you want to follow him when he next goes outside.'

The opportunity eventually arose and, the Warden showing willingness, Badger stood once more on the borders of the Park, sniffing the air in all directions. The snow still lay packed on the ground, and the icy temperature cut at his pampered body like a knife. He half turned back, looking towards the open cottage door that symbolized the way through to comfort. Ginger Cat was sitting on the threshold. He stood up. 'I'll come with you part of the way,' he offered.

'Gladly,' replied Badger.

The Warden watched the two animals that had become fast friends walk slowly off. His job was done.

They skirted the Edible Frogs' pond and Badger remembered Toad and Adder were sleeping nearby, deep down in a bankside away from the weather. All they would know of the winter would be from the stories they would hear from their friends.

'I wonder how *they've* been?' Badger muttered to himself. Fox and Vixen, Mole, Weasel, Tawny Owl . . . his friends seemed as strangers. He had become more familiar of late with a human's pet than with his companions of old.

A little way further on Ginger Cat stopped. 'I'll turn back now,' he said. 'Go carefully. And my best wishes to Mole and the foxes.'

'Farewell,' said Badger. 'Your company has been delightful. I know we shall meet again.'

'Until then,' responded the cat.

Badger watched his sinewy form retrace its steps through the snow. The sky was leaden above the Park; the air still and threatening. A snowstorm was imminent. He must reach his set as quickly as possible. There would be plenty of time to see his friends tomorrow.

═══ 9 ═══
Old Friends, New Friends

The reticence Badger was feeling for re-adopting his old life and friends he himself would never had admitted – even if he had been conscious of it. But those same old friends noticed the change in him at once from *their* unchanged world. Mole, who had been haunting Badger's set regularly ever since the animals had heard of his whereabouts, entered the set through his connecting tunnel. At first he thought a strange badger had commandeered the place, his old friend looked – and smelt – so different.

'Oh! hallo, Mole,' Badger greeted him unenthusiastically, as his little friend stood hesitantly. 'Yes, it *is* me.'

'I've been keeping a look-out for your return for days,' Mole said. 'We've missed you so much. But it *was* kind of the Warden's cat to come all this way to put our minds at rest. I'm only sorry about the accident that occurred.'

'He certainly deserved a better reception,' Badger remarked rather coldly, to Mole's consternation. 'He only made the journey at all because I forced him into it, really. However, he asked to be remembered to you.'

'Thank you,' said Mole in a small voice. He did not like this new, gruff individual.

There was a silence for some moments. Badger did not seem at all disposed to carry on a conversation, and Mole was becoming timid.

'You – you look d-different,' he stammered. 'Sort of fatter.'

'I probably am,' Badger agreed shortly. 'I was fed well.'

'I'm g-glad,' Mole whispered. 'I'll go and tell Fox you're here,' he added, and moved away in a confused way.

'Don't bother yourself,' said Badger. 'I suppose I ought to go. Er – I'll see you later, Mole.'

The crestfallen Mole watched his friend disappear up the exit tunnel without so much as a backward glance.

Outside it was dark and a fresh fall of snow had covered the Park. Badger's face became grim and he gritted his teeth. The contrast between the stark world of the wild and the comfort of human habitation was heightened still further in his mind. On his way to Fox's earth he was spied by Tawny Owl, who skimmed down from an oak branch.

'Welcome back, old friend,' the bird said, eyeing Badger openly. 'You seem to have prospered during your spell under the Warden's roof. You've got plump – and soft.'

Badger shrugged. 'It was a welcome relief from staring starvation in the face,' he said.

'I can see that,' Tawny Owl responded sarcastically. 'It must make it all the more difficult to adjust back again.'

'Why do I have to?' Badger asked bluntly.

Tawny Owl feigned ignorance. 'What *do* you mean, Badger?'

'Come along with me to see Fox,' Badger told him, 'and I'll put you both in the picture.'

'Hm,' Tawny Owl muttered. 'This should prove to be a most interesting meeting.'

Fox's earth was deserted when they arrived, and Badger said he would wait for Fox and Vixen's return. So he made himself as comfortable as he could underground while Tawny Owl perched in a nearby holly tree. He found his thoughts straying back to that warm kitchen in the Lodge. He imagined his friend Ginger Cat curled up in his basket, secure in the knowledge that he could depend on being fed without even stirring out of doors, and quite oblivious of the icy clutch of Winter that still held imprisoned every inhabitant of the Park.

Yes, the ways of the Wild could be dreadfully hard, and the arrival of Fox and Vixen at that juncture gave an emphasis to Badger's conclusion. Their emaciated frames, rimed with frost from the freezing air, slunk into the den and slumped, exhausted, on the hard ground. Badger, shocked beyond his expectation, was speechless. Presently the pair of foxes revived sufficiently to greet him. Of the two, Fox seemed thinnest and the most spent, which suggested that the best of the pickings of their nightly forays were going to Vixen. That would be Fox's way, Badger knew.

But Fox had lost none of his shrewdness. There was a look in his eyes that seemed to penetrate to Badger's most secret thoughts. His words, too, went straight to the heart of the matter. 'Well, are you back with us now for good?' he asked.

The question made Badger feel ashamed – ashamed of his well-fed appearance, his spotless coat. He felt as if he had betrayed Fox in a way, even if only in his thoughts. He did not know how to answer.

'The other way of life seems to agree with you,' Fox continued in a parallel of Tawny Owl's remark.

'Well, Fox, you know, I *was* injured,' Badger said defensively, almost apologetically.

'Of course you were,' Fox said. 'I'm sorry. How is your leg? Are you fully recovered?'

'Absolutely, thank you,' Badger replied a little more brightly. 'But, my dear Fox – and Vixen – you look as if you are suffering dreadfully.'

'Things are very, very hard,' Fox admitted, shaking his head slowly from side to side. 'Each day is harder. Only two of the voles are still alive, and scarcely more of the fieldmice. Rabbit and his friends have lost four of their number, too. And the squirrels find it almost impossible to dig through this never-ending snow to reach their buried nuts and berries so, they too, are dwindling. I really don't know what's to become of us all. We shall *all* die, Badger, if this weather doesn't lift soon, I'm sure of it.'

Badger felt that now was the time to play his trump card. 'There *is* an answer,' he said quietly.

'Well, let's have it. We're at our wits' end.'

'You don't *have* to live in the Park,' Badger explained. 'Come back with me to the Warden's cottage.'

Fox and Vixen looked at him in amazement.

'You can't mean it, Badger?' Vixen spoke for the first time.

'Of course I mean it,' Badger insisted. 'Why are you looking at me in that way? I was looked after, fed properly, and restored to health – and now I'm fitter than I've been for ages.'

'But you were injured and found by the Warden,' Fox repeated to himself uncomprehendingly. 'The welfare of the creatures of the Park is his concern so, naturally, he nursed you until you were better.'

'Exactly!' cried Badger. 'You've said it yourself. So isn't *your* welfare, and the rabbits' welfare, and the voles' welfare, and everyone else's welfare also of interest to him?'

At this point Tawny Owl poked his head down the hole. He felt he was missing an interesting discussion and wanted to hear. Fox's voice was audible next.

'Are you suggesting, then,' he was saying in an incredulous tone, 'that all of us band together and follow you to the Warden's Lodge?'

'Yes, I am.'

'And then what would we do? All rush inside the next time he appears at the door?'

'I don't know exactly what plan we could make,' Badger allowed. 'But we could work something out. Ginger Cat might help us think of something. Don't you see, Fox, your worries about food would be over? You would have no need even to think about it. It would be provided for you automatically.'

Tawny Owl stepped into the den. He could not resist participating any longer. 'I think our friend Badger has spent a little too much time amongst domestic creatures like cats,' he said drily. 'He's beginning to talk like one of them.'

'I can't believe it's our Badger talking,' Vixen said. 'Whatever has happened to him?'

'Oh, why can't you understand?' Badger wailed. 'I'm thinking of your good. Look at you – you're half-starved. A few more weeks and there may not be any trace left of the animals of Farthing Wood. Is that what you want?'

'Badger, your wits have become softened by your dependence on human aid,' Tawny Owl told him. 'I believe you've forgotten how to think for yourself. How could all the creatures from Farthing Wood be accommodated in your precious Warden's house? Squirrels, rabbits, hares, foxes . . . he isn't running a zoo.'

'He would find a way, I'm sure,' Badger replied vaguely. 'He would *have* to, once he sees the pitiful state of you all. It's his job, isn't it?'

'You're not making sense, Badger. You seem to have forgotten all the *original* inhabitants of White Deer Park,' Fox reminded him. 'We're just a small part of the fauna here. What if they all decided to come too?'

'The whole idea is the most absurd thing I've ever heard,' Tawny Owl said bluntly. 'I'm sorry you were injured, Badger, but I'm more sorry you were ever taken into captivity. It seems to have turned your brain.'

'I didn't say anything about *you* coming,' Badger snapped irritably. 'You and Kestrel wouldn't be welcome. Ginger Cat will vouch for that.'

Fox and Tawny Owl exchanged glances. It really did seem as if Badger had undergone a change of character. Vixen tried to smooth things over. 'You'll feel differently when you've got used to your old life again, Badger,' she said soothingly. 'I can see you're finding it difficult to pick up the threads again, and that's understandable. We'll win through yet, if we all pull together. Think what you Farthing Wood animals have survived before. If any creatures can see it through, you can.'

Badger was furious at the rejection of his idea. He rounded on his old friends angrily. 'You don't understand,' he fumed. 'I don't want my old life anymore. I didn't have to come back, but I did – for you. If you won't join me, I'll go back alone.'

'Back to your new friend the cat, no doubt,' Tawny Owl said. 'He's really got to work on you, hasn't he?'

'The Warden is my friend, too,' Badger barked.

'Well, it's quite obviously a clear case of preference,' Tawny Owl told him. 'You must go where your inclinations direct you.'

'Sssh, Owl,' Fox warned him. 'This is getting out of hand.' He turned to Badger. 'My dear friend, you can't mean what you say. We've been inseparable. You can't turn your back on us now?'

'*You* turned your back on *me*,' Badger insisted with a glare. 'My suggestion was made in good faith. I can't force you to come. It's your choice. As far as I'm concerned, *I* have no intention of starving to death. If you all want to die together, I must leave you to it.' With that he turned and left the earth.

His three prior companions were stunned. None of them ventured a word. Fox went to the exit and peered out at the retreating figure. He wanted to call out, to bring him back, but he could think of nothing more to say. A cold shiver ran along his body. It had begun to snow again.

— 10 —
A Question of Loyalties

In the morning Mole arrived at the foxes' earth in a very piteous state. He had remained in the set where Badger had left him, hoping to see him again. But after the talk with Fox, Vixen and Tawny Owl, Badger had returned to his set in an unpleasant mood and had been very unkind to Mole.

'He told me I was a confounded nuisance and a sniveller, and that I must leave him in peace or suffer the consequences,' he sobbed to Fox.

Vixen intervened. 'You must accept that Badger's simply not himself at the moment, Mole,' she counselled. 'None of us understands exactly what's happened. But if he's still our Badger, sooner or later his real feelings will show through. I know they will.'

'Oh, do you think so, Vixen?' Mole wept. 'Oh, I hope so, I hope so . . . .'

'Has Badger gone back?' Fox asked Mole.

'Gone back where?' queried Mole who, of course, was unaware of the scene of the previous night.

Fox was obliged to explain. 'He wants to go back to the Warden. He can't face his old life any more.' He described the meeting with Badger in his earth.

'What ever can we do?' Mole shrilled. 'We can't just let him go.'

'Perhaps it's the best thing for us to do, at present,' Vixen said. 'Then he can get this new way of life out of his system. If I know Badger, very soon he will begin to feel very guilty indeed, and then he'll come to his senses.'

'I think we should inform everyone of this business,' said Fox, 'and the best way to do it is for us all to meet – everyone – in Badger's empty set. I'll get Tawny Owl and Kestrel to round all the animals up. It's too cold to meet in the Hollow.'

'When do we meet?' Mole wanted to know.

'This very day,' said Fox. 'You go·to the set now, Mole. I'll contact Kestrel. Vixen, will you speak to Owl? There must be no delay.'

While preparations were being made, Badger was well on his way across the Park to his destination. Already a slight sense of shame hung over him as he turned his back on the Farthing Wood animals' home area. But he also felt resentment of his treatment by Fox and Tawny Owl, and looked forward to Ginger Cat's commiserations.

He had not bothered to hunt for any food, because he knew the Warden could be relied on to look after his stomach. He saw Kestrel flying over the Park and hoped he would not notice him. In the case of Kestrel this was a vain hope, for the hawk did not miss much that moved on the ground. Badger watched him swoop down.

'Well, what do you want?' Badger grunted ungraciously. 'I suppose you've come to insult me as well?'

'Not at all, not at all,' Kestrel declared indignantly. 'Fox has sent me to round up all our friends. I'm still looking for Weasel.'

'What for? A meeting?' Badger asked uninterestedly.

'Yes. No need to guess what it's about.'

'Me, I suppose? Well, I'm not surprised. But listen, Kestrel, tell Fox from me not to interfere. I can live where I choose. You must know as well as I do *they'll* all be dead inside a month the way things are going.'

'Not if I can help it,' Kestrel replied quickly. 'I hunt outside the Park every day and bring back what I can for them. And I know Whistler does too. Of course, at night Tawny Owl does what he can. *We* haven't forgotten the Oath.'

Badger looked away, a little shamefaced, at this pointed rejoinder. But he would not turn back. 'I wish you all well,' he said, 'but when the solution to your problems was offered it was refused. *I* can't be blamed.'

Kestrel directed one of his piercing glares at Badger and flew away resignedly. But later that day, he and Badger were due to meet again in very different circumstances.

Ginger Cat was sitting by the Warden's fence, blinking dozily in a few brief moments of sunlight that had managed to penetrate the clouds. Badger called him as he saw him. He expected the cat to come towards him, but he did not move. He called again. 'Hallo – it's me – Badger!'

Ginger Cat looked at him enigmatically. 'So I see,' he said coolly.

Badger stopped in his tracks, completely taken aback by this most unexpected lack of enthusiasm. 'Whatever's the matter?' he asked. 'I thought you would be pleased to see me.'

'I'm surprised to see you again at all so soon,' murmured Ginger Cat, yawning widely.

'But I've come back,' Badger explained. 'You know – for good.'

The cat looked at him long and steadily. 'What do you mean – for good?'

'I've made my decision, and I'm going to live with you.'

'What *are* you talking about? You live underground, you told me.'

'No, no, not any more. I'm finished with all that. I don't want that sort of existence. I've left my old friends because they wouldn't come with me.'

'Of course they wouldn't,' Ginger Cat said. 'I never expected them to. I thought all those pie-in-the-sky ideas of yours would be forgotten once you'd got back to your real home.'

These last words really jarred on Badger's sensibility. 'But I have a new home now . . . or I thought I had,' he faltered. 'Don't you remember, we talked about the Warden looking after Fox and Mole and everyone?'

'Indeed I do,' the cat answered. 'But I would have been astonished in the extreme if your wild friends chose of their own accord to leave their homes. Would *you* have come here if you hadn't been brought?'

'Er – no, I suppose not,' Badger admitted. 'But that doesn't matter. *I've* chosen this way of life.'

'How convenient for you,' Ginger Cat observed bitingly.

'*Aren't* you pleased to see me?' the bewildered Badger cried. 'I thought we were friends.'

'Oh yes,' the cat shrugged. 'But we were forced into each other's company, after all. One makes the most of a situation.'

'Well – er – aren't you going to invite me in?' Badger asked hesitantly.

'You're too bulky to go through my cat flap,' Ginger Cat pointed out. 'You'll have to wait for the man to find you. But I don't think you'll get the reaction you want from him. He looked after you until you were well again and, in his view, you should now be living in your natural state.'

'We'll see about that,' Badger answered hotly, but he was beginning to feel he had made a fool of himself. He went and sat by the front door and, as luck would have it, the Warden appeared soon after. A cry of amazement escaped him as he saw his old charge looking hopefully up at him. He bent down, examined the healed leg, patted Badger, and looked at him in a puzzled way for a moment. Then he seemed to think of something and turned back inside. Badger immediately tried to follow him, but the Warden kindly, but firmly, pushed him back and shut the door. Badger was heart-broken.

'You see,' Ginger Cat's soft voice purred at him. 'He doesn't want you any more. Oh, he'll probably bring you a bowl of food in a minute or two. He imagines you've come for that. But your home is not his cottage any more.'

The realization of his stupidity flashed into Badger's mind in a blinding flood of light. What a miscalculation he had made! *He* was not a domestic animal. How could he have thought he understood human ways? Both the cat and the human were on another plane of existence, in a world he could never comprehend. He had humiliated himself, and in the process he had lost the respect of the cat and, what was worse – far worse! – spurned his real friends.

The bowl of food predicted by Ginger Cat was brought
out, and a dish of warm milk with it. More to save the
Warden a disappointment than because of any feeling
of appetite, Badger ate and drank. Then, with a wry
look at the cat, he turned back without a further word
– back to his waiting set.

A short distance from the cottage he looked behind
him. The Warden was not to be seen, but Ginger Cat
was still sitting, watching his retreat. Badger heard a
flutter of wings above and Kestrel alighted beside him.

'Keep going, Badger,' he told him. 'You're going in
the right direction this time.'

Badger knew the hawk had guessed what had hap-
pened and smiled sadly at him. 'Yes, Kestrel,' he whis-
pered, 'I have indeed been a foolish creature.'

Behind them, unknown to them, Ginger Cat had spot-
ted his enemy. Now, belly flat to the icy ground, he was
creeping stealthily forward on his noiseless feet. With a
tremendous spurt, he leapt on the unsuspecting hawk,
teeth and claws as sharp as razors finding their mark.
But Kestrel was no sparrow or blackbird. He was a
hunter, a killer himself, and his powerful wings flailed,
beating against his assailant, while his lethal beak darted
in all directions in an attempt to strike.

Badger looked round in horror. The bird, taken un-
awares, was struggling desperately against the attack.
Badger was hopelessly torn between his affection for the
cat, albeit recently somewhat battered, and his loyalty
to an old friend. He could see Kestrel's struggles weak-
ening and, in a trice, it was as if a veil had been lifted
from his eyes. The Oath!

Badger rushed into the fray. Bringing all his consider-
able weight and power into the attack he fell on Ginger
Cat, lunging with bared teeth at his throat. The cat let

out a scream and spat at him in fury. But the grip was loosened and Kestrel was able to free himself, flying up into the air instantly.

Now the fight was left to the two animals, and soon Badger's superior strength began to tell. He knew the cat was at his mercy and that one snap of his jaws could kill him. His instinct told him to do it, but he held back. Although he had made the cat party to the Oath, the animal had forfeited his right to protection by attacking another of its adherents. But Badger recalled the good turn Ginger Cat had done him and now he must repay it. He stepped away, his sides heaving, and, like an arrow, the cat sped away, back to safety.

The significance of Badger's rescue was not lost on Kestrel. 'Welcome back to the fold,' he screeched from the air.

'It's quite safe for you now,' Badger called back. 'Come down and let me see if you're injured.'

Kestrel did so and Badger noticed the marks of the cat's claws. He began to lick at his friend's body.

'Most obliged,' said the hawk. 'Thanks for your help. For just a moment I wondered if you were going to.'

'I know,' said Badger. 'Oh, what a supreme idiot I've been. I've entered unknown waters and found myself out of my depth. It's so absurd. I'd rather die *with* you all than live without you.'

'We *won't* die,' Kestrel insisted. 'It's going to be tough, but we are tough creatures.'

'They're not deep scratches,' Badger was saying. 'They'll soon heal.'

'Er – Badger – why did you let the cat go?'

Badger explained.

'I thought as much. That means I still have him after my blood.'

'Just stay in the air in this vicinity,' Badger told him. 'But the cat will know why I didn't kill him and that my debt is repaid. He has a fair nature. I don't think he will be out for revenge any more.'

'I hope you're right,' said Kestrel. 'Well, if you hurry, you will surprise the rest of them holding forth about you in your set.'

'I'll see you there,' Badger replied.

11

An Expedition

The meeting of the animals of Farthing Wood to discuss Badger's strange behaviour and what should be done about it had not long begun when Kestrel arrived. He saw Whistler standing at the entrance to the set.

'Are you on guard?' he asked the heron.

'No. My legs are too long for me to go in there.' He pointed with his long bill to the entrance tunnel.

'In that case,' said Kestrel, 'you'll be the first to know that Badger is himself again.' He went on to describe his rescue from Ginger Cat.

'That *will* delight everyone,' Whistler said. 'You go in and tell them before Tawny Owl runs him down too much.' He winked elaborately.

Kestrel walked into the set. As he joined the meeting,

it was evident that Tawny Owl was replying to a suggestion from someone that they should bring Badger back by force.

'What for?' he hooted. 'Leave him to his own devices. He turned his back on us. Why should we bother any longer?'

'You're beginning to talk just like Adder,' said Mole. 'It would be wrong of us to desert him.'

'That's just what he's done to us,' snorted Owl.

'Two wrongs don't make a right,' Mole replied, rather weakly.

'You can all save your breath,' Kestrel informed them. 'Badger's on his way back.'

They looked at him dumbfounded. Then he explained again about Badger's change of heart and his rescue.

'You see, Mole,' Vixen said kindly, 'I knew his real character would win through.'

'Oh, *I* never lost faith in him,' Mole declared proudly, while Tawny Owl looked rather abashed. 'Dear Badger! So he came to help you, Kestrel?'

'He saved my life,' Kestrel said honestly. 'No question about it.'

'I'm very happy,' said Fox. 'I feel that this heralds an improvement in our affairs. Well, Kestrel, should we stay for him?'

'Oh yes!' answered Kestrel emphatically. 'Now we're all together. He's depending on seeing us.'

'So be it,' said Fox and the animals settled down to wait patiently.

Late in the afternoon Badger greeted Whistler outside his home. He paused at the set entrance nervously, unsure of his other friends' reception.

'Oh, you're a hero again,' Whistler reassured him. 'Kestrel has told them all about it.'

Badger smiled and, taking a deep breath, went to meet his fate.

He need not have worried. Most of the animals had not seen him since his accident and received him like a long-lost friend. Mole was in raptures, Fox and Vixen relieved, and even Tawny Owl gave him a gruff, 'Glad to see you, Badger.'

A tacit understanding seemed to exist on both sides not to mention Badger's recent aberration, and all was forgotten. But Badger gloomily noticed the depletion in numbers of the little band that had set out the previous spring to look for their new home. Leaving aside the absence of the hibernating hedgehogs, Toad and Adder, there were gaps in the ranks of the squirrels and the rabbits, while Vole was accompanied only by his own mate and Fieldmouse by just two others of his family. Of the rest, lean bodies and hungry eyes told their tale. Only Mole, apart from himself, seemed unchanged.

Fox followed Badger's gaze. 'The winter has not left us unscathed,' he summarised.

'No.' Badger shook his head sadly. 'But perhaps we should turn the meeting towards a more positive course. Unscathed we are not, but we should now plan how we can emerge from the season undefeated.'

'For many of us that call is too late,' Vole said bitterly.

'Then let us resolve to lose no more,' Badger responded.

'There's not a lot that can be done,' Fox said with untypical pessimism. The winter had taken its toll of spirit, too.

'Fox has done everything possible for him to do,' Hare added loyally. 'But none of us can control the weather conditions. When the entire Park lies buried under two feet of snow, it needs more than animal ingenuity to cope with the situation.'

'Let me tell you,' said Badger quietly, 'I think we really do need help from another source.'

'Are you thinking again along the same lines we all think you are thinking?' asked Weasel cryptically.

'No.' Badger replied at once. 'Not the Warden. But I *am* thinking about human help.' He looked round at his companions whose faces had, for the most part, dropped.

'Only it would be help,' he intoned slowly to emphasize his words, 'that the humans wouldn't know they were giving.'

'Whatever can you mean, Badger?' Rabbit asked.

'Well, listen. Now it's well-known that humans waste as much of their food as they eat. Why, then, shouldn't we make use of what they don't want?'

'I could never bring myself to resort to scavenging,' Tawny Owl said, rustling his wings importantly.

'Don't be pompous, Owl,' Badger said. 'When the other choice is starvation you should be ready to resort to anything.'

'Badger's quite right,' agreed Fox. 'We must consider any plan that will keep us alive. Please explain further, Badger.'

'You'll remember that Toad told us the story of his travels. Well, on the other side of the Park, not far from the boundary fence, there are human habitations and gardens. It was from one of those very gardens that he actually began his long journey back to Farthing Wood. And somewhere in those gardens, you can count on it, we will come across some of those tall things they put their unwanted food in.'

'You've certainly hit on something,' Fox conceded. 'But it will be a great way, and few of us are now strong enough to travel great distances. For the smaller animals it is completely out of the question.'

'I'll go,' said Badger. 'I'm the fittest of all at present. And the birds can go with me. Then they can carry back anything of use I find. Of course, if anyone else feels able to join me, I'd be delighted.'

'I shall accompany you, naturally,' said Fox.

Badger looked at his wasted form with misgiving. He knew Fox felt that in any such venture it was his duty to attend. 'Well, Fox, you know,' Badger said awkwardly, 'are you sure that – '

'That I'm strong enough?' Fox anticipated him. 'Of course I am. I should never forgive myself if I stayed behind.'

'There is never any doubt about your being brave enough anyway,' Vixen said lovingly and nuzzled him.

So it was arranged that Fox, Badger, Tawny Owl, Kestrel and Whistler would form the expedition. It would be essential to travel in the dark, so they decided they must go at the very first opportunity, which was that very night.

'How I wish Toad was around to direct us,' Fox said.

'Couldn't we dig him up?' Mole suggested. 'I bet I could reach him.'

Badger laughed. 'Impossible, I'm afraid, Mole,' he told him. 'You'd get no sense out of him. He's in his winter sleep and nothing will wake him up except a rise in temperature. In fact, to expose him suddenly to these temperatures would probably kill him.'

'Oh dear, I hadn't thought of that,' said Mole.

'I remember he mentioned a ditch on the other side of the fence,' Fox mused. 'If we can find that, and then that first road he travelled down from his captor's garden, we should make it all right.'

'Leave it to me,' offered Tawny Owl. 'I'll find you your ditch – and the road.'

'How long will it take you to cross the Park?' asked Fieldmouse. 'It must be miles.'

'It would be no problem at all if it weren't for the fact that we are so hampered by snow,' said Fox. 'But we must reach the houses while it's still dark. It should be dusk now. I suggest we start straight away.'

The others agreed and, without further ado, Fox and Badger with Tawny Owl and Kestrel, made their way out of the chamber to assorted cries of 'Good luck!' Outside the set they acquainted Whistler with their idea, and he was delighted to be of use.

Fox and Badger went, shoulder to shoulder, across the snowy waste in the direction of the Reserve's far fence. Kestrel and Whistler fluttered slowly in the unaccustomed darkness for short distances while they waited for the two animals to catch them up. Tawny Owl the night bird flew on ahead on silent wings to locate the ditch that was their marker.

'What do you expect to find?' Fox asked Badger.

Badger found it strange to be in the role of leader, which at present he clearly was. 'Oh, I don't know. Meat and vegetable scraps – there could be all sorts of things,' he answered vaguely. Then he wished he had not spoken, for he saw the eager look in the famished Fox's eyes and his mouth begin to water.

'It really has hit you hard, hasn't it, old friend?' he whispered to him. For a time Fox did not answer, and Badger wondered if he had heard. Then Fox spoke.

'It's been the hardest trial I've ever faced,' he said wearily. 'Harder than anything we faced on our journey here, including the Hunt.'

'It is so sad that, after the triumph of overcoming

every hazard en route to reach our new home, so many of our friends have perished before they really had a chance to enjoy their new life.'

'It *is* sad,' agreed Fox, 'but there is no doubt that old age has played its part. The life span of a mouse is very short.'

'But the rabbits? The squirrels?'

'I know, I know. It's not the start to our new life I had envisaged,' Fox muttered. 'But then, how many would have survived staying behind in Farthing Wood? If we get through the rest of the winter without losing any more of our numbers, there will be a breeding stock, at any rate, of all the animals to ensure a permanent representation of the Farthing Wood party in the Park.'

'Except in one or two cases,' Badger said, smiling sadly.

'I'm sorry, Badger,' Fox said awkwardly. 'I really put my foot in it. I wasn't thinking.'

'Don't worry. I know what you meant. And it seems our priority must be to save Vole and Fieldmouse at all costs.'

'That is so,' said Fox. 'And that's where the difficulty lies. The White Deer herd have, on occasion, brought some of their hay for our vegetarians to eat. The problem is, the mice don't really like stalks. It's the seeds they want. And berries and insects. Of course, they're virtually unobtainable.'

'Well,' said Badger, 'perhaps we'll find something for them.'

When they next caught up with the birds, Tawny Owl was waiting as well. He told them he had found the ditch and the road down which they must go.

'Did you find the houses, too?' asked Badger.

'Er – yes,' he replied uncertainly.

'What's wrong?' asked Fox.

'Well, we shall all have to be cautious,' he explained. 'It seems there are others around on the same errand.'

—12—
A Raid

'Foxes?'

'Yes, a pair.'

'Where?'

'Along the road.'

'Well, we aren't the only creatures in the Park who are suffering. We sometimes tend to forget that.'

'How do we know they're from the Park?' Kestrel mentioned.

'True,' admitted Fox. 'But it's most likely.'

Before they reached the boundary of the Park, he asked to have a brief rest. Badger's concerned expression was unconcealed. 'I'll be all right,' Fox assured them all. 'I've lost a little of my strength, I'm afraid.'

Eventually they reached the fence and found a spot

where previous animals had scooped away the ground underneath in order to come and go as they pleased. Badger and Fox scrambled underneath and crossed the ditch. Tawny Owl led them to the road.

The surface was like glass where motor traffic had beaten down the falls of snow into a tight mass. But it was quiet now and empty. The animals padded slowly along it until the first of the human dwellings was reached.

'Wait here,' said Tawny Owl. 'I'll investigate.' Badger and Fox hid themselves in the darkest spot against the garden wall, while Whistler and Kestrel perched high up on a chimney pot.

'This one's no good,' Tawny Owl later informed them. 'The wall is too high for you and so are the gates.' They moved on to the next house to find the same problem. Fox looked at Badger significantly.

'Owl!' Badger called in a low voice. 'See if you can find the other foxes again. Perhaps they know something we don't.'

Tawny Owl returned with astonishing news. He had located the strange foxes in the grounds of a large house some distance away from the others. They had simply jumped the comparatively low fence and were nosing around a number of sheds and hutches. From sounds he had heard, Owl had discovered that one of these was a chicken coop, and this was obviously the foxes' target.

'Chickens!' exclaimed Fox.

'The same,' said Tawny Owl.

'But the racket! They'll wake the entire neighbourhood.' Despite his protestations, Fox was having the utmost difficulty in preventing himself from drooling. The thought of food had an overwhelming effect on him.

'There might be enough for all of us,' Badger hinted.

'What? You can't mean it, Badger. You wouldn't con-

done such – ' Fox broke off. He knew he was blustering;
playing a part – and so did Badger. For it had been the
first thought to cross his mind, too. After all, in strai-
tened circumstances, one has to consider any opening.

'I wonder how they get them out?' Badger muttered.

'Come and see,' Tawny Owl said.

They followed him further along the road, the other
birds accompanying. Owl perched on the fence he had
told them about.

'There's certainly a strong scent of fox,' said Badger.

'And also of chickens,' Fox whispered.

'Carefully now,' Tawny Owl warned the two animals
as he, Kestrel and Whistler fluttered into the grounds.

Fox and Badger looked at the fence. 'Can you jump
it?' Badger asked.

'If I were fully fit – nothing easier. But a lot of my
stamina's gone. However, I'll have a jolly good try.
What about you?'

'*I'm* no jumper,' answered Badger. 'You go ahead,
and I'll scout round the outside of the fence and see if
there's another way in. I'll join you inside.'

He watched Fox backing away from the fence in order
to give himself a good run up to it. Then he saw him
leap upwards, just scraping the fence-top, before he
landed the other side. Badger was now alone on the road
side of the fence. He shuffled along its length, looking
for a suitable opening. But there seemed to be no way
through. There was a gate halfway along one side which,
of course, was closed. He paused, wondering whether he
should call out. Just then there broke out the most appal-
ling din. There was a loud crash, immediately followed
by the most frenzied squawks and a clattering of wings.
Badger correctly surmised that one of the foxes was
attempting to break in to the coop. The noise grew

absolutely deafening, and then he heard a barking and human shouts.

Cowering against the fence, not knowing if he should stay or run, Badger saw two foxes leap the fence into the road, a hen dangling from each of their pairs of jaws. Then they were off, racing down the road as fast as their burdens would allow them. Suddenly he heard three or four gunshots in quick succession and a very scared third fox – his own friend – leapt the fence almost on top of him.

'Quick!' Fox shouted hoarsely. 'This way!' And he raced away in the opposite direction to that taken by the two raiders. Badger sloped after him as fast as he could go – and in the nick of time. Out of the gate in the fence came a huge, ferocious and furious dog followed by two men – one young, one elderly – each with shotguns. The dog instantly set off after the foxes carrying the chickens. These animals were badly hampered by their heavy loads and the dog gained on them quickly. But the two men were taking aim with their guns. One called the dog, which checked its headlong rush, and then two more shots rang out. The two foxes dropped like stones and rolled over in the snow, the maimed chickens flapping helplessly in the gutter.

The men went to examine the fox carcasses, and seemed satisfied with their work. The younger one put the injured chickens out of their misery, and picked them up by their feet. The dog pranced around him, tongue lolling and tail wagging.

From their hiding-place under a parked car, Badger and Fox watched the men and their dog trudge back to the garden, their hearts beating wildly. Only when the gate in the fence had once again been fastened after them did they dare to move.

'Phew!' gasped Fox who really had felt in fear of his life. 'That was a little *too* close for my liking.'

'Yes,' Badger agreed. 'It's certainly a good thing we hadn't reached that garden first.'

'But I don't know if I should have tried what those poor devils did anyway,' Fox confessed. 'I've never been one for taking such prey.'

'Maybe they were desperate like us,' Badger suggested pointedly.'

Fox ignored him. 'Where are the birds?' he asked.

Tawny Owl was the first to find them. 'So much for your ideas of invading gardens,' he said to Badger crossly. 'Could have had us all killed.'

'*You* were the one to tell us about the chickens,' said Badger. 'We still haven't investigated my suggestion.'

'I don't think I could go back in there again,' Fox said. 'Is the coast clear now, Owl?'

'No,' he replied. 'Those foxes turned the coop over and the stupid hens are running all over the place. The men will have their work cut out collecting them together again.'

'Give them time,' said Badger. 'After coming all this way we can't go back with nothing.'

'Will you keep us informed please, Owl?' Fox asked. 'Badger and I will wait here.'

'Can't see the point,' muttered Tawny Owl. 'Badger can't get into the garden anyway.'

Badger looked at Fox. 'This garden is our only chance,' he said. 'It's the only one with a fence. Are you sure you couldn't make just one more jump?'

Fox wavered. It seemed as if he was fated always to be the one on whom everyone else depended.

'You know I would gladly go if I could get in,' Badger added. 'But I've looked all round for a hole and there's just nothing.'

Fox smiled a little smile of resignation. 'It looks as if I have no choice really, doesn't it?' he said.

So Tawny Owl flew back to watch the proceedings, and Fox and Badger huddled together under the car again to wait. Some time passed and they heard nothing. Badger was restless. 'I think I'll just wander a little further along this road just in case there's anything of interest,' he told his companion.

He had not been gone long when Fox heard a familiar whistle in the air, and then saw the long thin legs of Whistler standing by the car. He emerged from his hideaway.

'Ah, there you are,' said the heron. 'I've some excellent news for you. The men have hung the dead chickens up in a shed and I think, if you really make yourself as flat as possible you could get under the door. There's a gap just about wide enough for you.'

Fox's ears pricked up. 'Things are looking up,' he replied. 'Is all quiet again?'

'The men have set all to rights and returned inside,' Whistler answered.

'And the dog?'

'Er – chained to a kennel,' said Whistler. 'But I'm sure you can handle him.'

'What are you saying?' cried Fox in exasperation. 'Am I, in my state, a match for a dog of that size?'

'Not physically, of course,' said the heron calmly. 'But we all know of your powers of persuasion.'

'I'm afraid you must have too high an opinion of me,' Fox returned, shaking his head. 'You may have heard of a previous exploit of mine, regarding a bull-mastiff – a stupid dog. But this situation is altogether different. This dog, whatever it is, is twice the size with twice the strength whereas I – well, you have only to look at me.'

'You are indeed underweight,' Whistler acknowl-

edged. 'But that is to be expected. Are you saying your
mental faculties have been affected by the winter?'

'It's a question of spirit and courage – and the will to
do something,' Fox said wearily. 'I'm simply not the
same animal any more. On the journey from Farthing
Wood I had plenty of spirit. Determination, too. I had
a *purpose*. It's different now.

'But, my dear Fox,' Whistler said with a worried look.
'I can't bear to hear you talk like this. You, above all
my friends, have always been an example of tenacity
and resourcefulness and resolution to look up to. You
inspired the others – you still do. And surely you *still*
have a purpose. To survive. Think of Vixen if not of
yourself.'

For a moment something of the old look returned to
Fox's poor haggard face. He was thinking of what he
had been like when Vixen had first encountered him.
The pitiful shadow of himself that he now was would
never have won her regard and admiration as he had
then. Then his eyes glazed over again.

'No, it's no use, Whistler,' he said lamely. 'I'm sorry
if I'm letting you down but I'm beaten before I start.
I'll simply wilt in front of that monster.'

Whistler was really alarmed at Fox's lack of motiva-
tion. Even his mention of Vixen had not done the trick.
He flew back to Tawny Owl and Kestrel for advice.

'Yes, he's taken things very hard,' Kestrel said when
the heron had related his conversation.

'Humph!' snorted Tawny Owl. 'I believe in calling
things by their proper name. His spirit is completely
broken, and he's no longer the brave leader we once
knew.'

'How can we help him?' asked Whistler. 'It's awful to
see him cowering in the road under that car.'

'Only a full stomach and the arrival of Spring can help him now,' said Tawny Owl. 'He's a beaten animal.'

Unbeknown to the three birds, the subject of their discussion had crept up to the garden fence and could overhear every word. If the scene had been pre-arranged it could not have had a better result. Fox's pride, battered as it was, refused to accept the verdict of Tawny Owl, and his body visibly stiffened. He thought again of Vixen and what it would mean to her if he failed. He could not bear to sink in her estimation. He pulled himself more erect and backed away from the fence.

The birds were still talking when they saw him leap the fence for the third time, but with an added grace that made them fall silent. He went warily across the centre of the grounds of the house, giving the re-established chicken coop a wide berth. He saw the dog, half in and half out of the kennel, with its head on its paws, and he approached cautiously step by step. Having convinced himself that it was dozing, Fox looked around for the shed Whistler had described to him. He soon found it.

In his emaciated state it was no problem for him to crawl under the door. The chickens were hanging by the feet from nails in the side of the shed. Fox pulled one free and backed under the gap again. Here he met with a difficulty for the chicken got caught. However, with a backward tug, he wrenched it free and ran back to the fence.

The birds fully expected him to jump the fence and be satisfied with his good luck. But Fox had evidently decided to do things in style. He dropped the chicken, then loped back to the shed and scrambled under the door again. All this time the dog had not stirred a muscle. Fox found the second hen to be much larger and needed two pulls to bring it to the ground. Back he came under the shed door and then the larger hen became firmly wedged. Fox tugged it this way and that, but its plump body would not shift. Whistler was on the point of flying over to tell Fox that perhaps it would be best to be content with one and to get away while the going was good, when Badger's voice was heard calling beyond the fence.

'Fox! Owl! Are you there?' he was saying.

'We're here,' hissed Tawny Owl from his branch. 'Be quiet. The dog's asleep.'

'I've found a regular dump of food,' he called back excitedly, regardless of the warning. 'At the end of the road. Come and look.'

Kestrel flew over to the fence and perched on the top. 'Wait a moment, Badger,' he whispered. 'Fox is in the grounds collecting chickens.'

Badger's jaw dropped. He could not comprehend that Kestrel was referring to the two dead ones. 'He must be mad!' he cried. 'Does he want to commit suicide?'

Kestrel calmed him down. 'It's not what you think,' he said. 'We'll explain later.'

Fox had given the second chicken a particularly vicious wrench and it was almost free. But at that moment the dog awoke and yawned widely. It stood up, shaking its body vigorously. Fox heard the sound and froze. How far did that chain stretch? He peered round the side of the shed. The dog was some twenty feet away, but Fox had no idea if it could reach him if it made a lunge. He waited. The dog began to sniff the snow all round its kennel. It found something of interest and sniffed harder, running in looping patterns through the snow, its nose always on the ground. Fox watched it go to the full length of its chain in the direction opposite to where he was standing and gulped as he saw how far it stretched. If it came his way it could easily reach him. He waited no longer. He heaved the chicken free and ran almost in front of the dog as it was returning on the axis of the chain's length. It saw him and immediately started to bark again.

Fox raced for the fence and cleared it easily. 'Take this!' he cried as he dropped the chicken on the road side of the fence by Badger. Then, incredibly, in the teeth of danger he backed away for yet another jump. The dog was barking incessantly as Fox leapt the fence again to snap up the chicken he had left behind. Lights were appearing once more in the house. But Fox was up and over the fence for the last time with the second chicken in his jaws. Without hesitation he took the opposite direction to that taken by the first two foxes, leaving poor Badger to struggle after him with the heavier hen. Tawny Owl, Kestrel and Whistler swooped over the fence behind them.

'The Park's that way!' called Tawny Owl. 'You're going in the wrong direction!' But Fox did not seem to hear.

Badger had no idea what Fox had in mind, but he gamely followed him as quickly as he could, expecting every minute to find the huge dog bearing down on him from behind. But though the deafening barking continued, no dog – nor men – appeared. Then suddenly the noise ceased. It seemed as if this is what Fox had been expecting, for he immediately stopped running and dropped the chicken, the better to take some deep breaths while he waited for Badger to catch him up.

'Not a bad haul, eh?' he said coolly to his friends as they bunched together. He seemed his old self.

'I don't understand,' said Badger.

'Understand what?'

'Why we weren't chased,' Badger panted.

'It's obvious,' Fox confided. 'When the men came out

of the house the second time they expected to see their chicken coop overturned again. As soon as they saw it intact, with no more chickens missing, they assumed the dog's barking had driven off any further prowlers. How could they know I knew about the dead hens in the shed?'

'Bravo, Fox. You're to be congratulated,' said Whistler. 'And you've proved you're still a shade sharper than most of us.'

Tawny Owl disliked anyone to be overpraised when he considered he had exceptional abilities himself. 'Oh well,' he said huffily, 'when you're down as low as you can be, you can only go upwards.'

The others glared at him but Fox, in his new-found confidence, only chuckled.

'Yet a little cunning can go a long way,' he said.

Live and Let Live

Badger was delighted at Fox's reinstatement as the animals' resourceful leader, and Whistler politely failed to mention that the idea of stealing the dead chickens had been his.

'I also have found something of interest,' Badger then announced.

'Ah yes – your discovery,' murmured Kestrel. 'What is it?'

'I hope it's something of value to our smaller friends,' said Fox. 'We mustn't forget that we still have nothing for *them*, and that is why I didn't turn back for the Park.'

'Well, come and see,' said Badger excitedly. 'There's everything we need.'

'How far is it?' Fox wanted to know. 'I feel quite worn out.'

'Of course you are, jumping backwards and forwards over that fence all those times – without mentioning the journey here. But it's not far along the road. We've run most of the way already.'

'You take the others with you, and show them what you want them to carry back,' Fox suggested. 'I'll wait here and take a breather and look after the chickens.'

So Badger, accompanied by the three birds, proceeded to the end of the road, where in fact a small general store that served the neighbourhood was situated. To the rear of the shop was a yard where discarded cartons, packets and unwanted stocks abounded. Amongst this was enough greenstuff to feed all the rabbits and hares comfortably, wasted bags of mixed nuts left over from Christmas and even quantities of pet food such as millet sprays for cage birds. Badger seemed to think the voles and fieldmice might like the latter, while the squirrels would be delighted by the nuts.

What would have been the astonishment of any human awake at that hour and looking on, to see a small aerial procession of a hawk, an owl and a heron on their way back to the Nature Reserve carrying their assorted gifts? Kestrel led the way with a collection of millet sprays in his pointed beak, then came Tawny Owl, a little self-consciously, laden with string bags of nuts – one in his beak and one clutched in his talons – and finally Whistler, his huge bill stuffed with cabbage leaves and a selection of greenery.

Badger watched them on their way and then rejoined Fox. 'I thought you might have indulged in a mouthful or two while you were waiting,' he said, referring to the chickens, 'just to keep your strength up.'

'No,' said Fox. 'We shall all feast together when we

get back to the Park. You and I and Vixen and Weasel.
And, of course, Owl and Kestrel, though I know Whis-
tler prefers fish. But first we have a journey ahead of us.'

Dawn was threatening to break as they went back
along the road, Fox now carrying the larger chicken.
They passed the scene of the raid and then the two dead
foxes. Now they were just stiff corpses in the snow, lying
where they had dropped and staining its whiteness with
their blood.

'These hens should have been theirs by rights,' Fox
muttered as he paused briefly at the sight. 'It could have
been Vixen and me.' Then they went on, crossed the
ditch, and re-entered the Park at the same point.

It was well on into the morning when the two animals,
after frequent stops to rest from their loads, arrived back
at Badger's set.

'Will you eat with me?' Badger asked, 'or shall I come
and join you and Vixen?'

'Just as you like,' Fox said wearily.

'May I suggest the set then?' said Badger, aware that
it offered considerably more comfort than the sparseness
of the foxes' earth.

'I must have a nap first,' Fox said decidedly. 'I'll help
you take our quarry underground, and then I'll be back
when it's dark, with Vixen.'

'I'm tired too,' agreed Badger as they deposited the
chickens in a safe place. 'But it was well worth the effort,
wasn't it?'

'Without a doubt,' replied Fox.

Later that day Fox, Badger, Vixen, Weasel, Tawny
Owl and Kestrel were together in Badger's set. There
was plenty to eat for all, and each of them felt it was the
first good meal they had had in a long while. Kestrel
informed Fox and Badger that he, Owl and Whistler
had made several trips back and forth to the food dump

and that all the animals had eaten well and were feeling a lot more cheerful.

'I really believe that Badger's brainwave will prove to be our salvation,' Fox said optimistically. Vixen looked at her mate lovingly. She had heard the tale of Fox's courage and cunning from Kestrel and was prouder of him than ever.

'It certainly seems that Badger's stay with humankind has produced some useful thinking,' remarked Tawny Owl.

'Owl and I and the heron can make regular flights to pick up more supplies,' said Kestrel. 'With just a little luck our depleted party should be around to welcome the spring.'

'But what of all of *us*?' Weasel demanded. 'Where do the supplies for the meat-eaters come from? Those small birds killed by the cold we sometimes pick up don't make a proper meal.'

All were silent, faced with a problem none of them had really considered. Badger thought of Ginger Cat's rats but diplomatically decided to say nothing.

'There can be no more raids on chicken coops,' said Fox. 'That would be suicidal.'

'Was there no meat amongst the wasted food?' Vixen asked.

'I have to admit we didn't really look,' said Kestrel. 'But that is easily remedied.'

'Perhaps, Owl, you could investigate tomorrow night?' Fox suggested.

'Perhaps I could, perhaps I couldn't,' he answered grumpily. 'I may have other plans.'

'Don't worry – I'll go,' said Kestrel in disgust. 'I can fly there in the daytime. No-one will notice a hovering hawk.'

'I didn't say I *wouldn't* go,' Tawny Owl rejoined. 'If you had waited, I no doubt would have offered.'

'Can't bear to be *asked* to do anything,' Kestrel muttered. 'Pompous old – '

He was interrupted by an unearthly scream outside the set.

'Whatever's that?' he cried.

'Have you never heard the scream of a captured hare?' Weasel asked.

'HARE!' they all shouted and Fox and Badger went racing for the exit. The others followed. Outside they smelt blood and Fox snuffled the crisp, icy air. 'This way!' he called. A little further off there was a patch of blood on the snow, and a trail of drops leading away from it. They followed and, eventually, found what they were looking for. Under a holly bush a stoat was devouring the limp body of a young hare. It looked up in alarm at the approaching group and quickly snatched up its prey, preparatory to flight.

'You needn't run,' said Fox. 'If that is one of our friends you have killed, we are too late. And, if not, we don't need the food.'

'I'm afraid it's one of the leverets, Hare's offspring,' Weasel announced.

'I have to eat, too, you know,' the stoat said defensively in a voice unnaturally shrill. 'I hunt what I can. N-no offence meant.'

'It's the law of the Wild,' said Badger. 'We mean you no harm.' He turned to the others. 'I met this fellow once before,' he said. 'Like us, he's finding it difficult to survive.'

'Of course,' said Fox. 'Who are we to complain?'

'What a strange world it is,' murmured Vixen. 'That poor little friend of ours came here, believing he had found safety, only to end up like this.'

The stoat was looking from one to the other, still unsure of its best action and half inclined to run.

'What's the difference?' Tawny Owl shrugged. 'He could as easily have been killed by the winter.'

'For most of us no home is without its dangers,' Fox observed. 'It's something we have to accept without question. However, my friend,' he continued, looking at the stoat, 'I wish you had hunted in another corner of the Park.'

The stoat seemed to sense it was safe now and increased in boldness. 'And you foxes – you hunt too. Where do you go in the Park to find food?'

'Yes, yes. We take the point,' answered Fox. 'Wherever we can find it – the same as you.'

'Never have I known such a winter,' the stoat went on. 'My mate has already died. I can see by your leanness you have suffered as well. But the badger seems very sleek.'

Badger shifted his stance a little uncomfortably.

'Yes, I saw you on another occasion,' the stoat said. 'You weren't so stout then. You must have been luckier than the rest of us.'

'If injuring myself severely can be called lucky, I have been,' Badger said enigmatically.

The stoat, of course, looked puzzled.

'He was discovered by the Warden and taken into care,' Weasel explained.

'A sort of fattening up process,' said Tawny Owl mischievously.

'All right, all right,' said Badger. 'Am I never to be allowed to forget it? Would you rather I hadn't been found and frozen to death?'

'Don't be absurd, Badger,' replied Tawny Owl. 'Nobody was more pleased than I at your recovery.'

'Well then, how much longer do I have to endure these carping comments?' Badger said irritably.

'Oh dear,' said the stoat grinning. 'The incident appears to be a bit of a bone of contention between you.'

'Let's drop the subject,' suggested Fox, 'and leave our friend here to eat in peace. And I sincerely hope Hare is nowhere at hand to overhear my remarks. He'd never forgive me.'

'I promise I'll endeavour to keep away from this area,' the stoat said agreeably. 'You've been more than polite.'

'Live and let live,' answered Fox. 'The Park belongs to all of us.'

He led the others away and they gradually dispersed to their own homes.

'H'm, quite a philosophical evening,' remarked Tawny Owl as he fluttered silently to his roost.

14
A New Danger

The winter wore relentlessly on, the old year fading into the new with no sign of change. The birds continued their trips to the food dump and were able to find a kind of meat – perhaps unwanted sausages or bacon or the like – to supplement what the meat-eaters were able to find in the Reserve. Now that the threat of imminent starvation had been lessened, the animals gritted their teeth, confident that it was now just a case of lasting out until the better weather came.

In other ways they were no more comfortable than before. They simply could not get used to the treacherous cold which never let up, nor the blizzards and snowfalls which occurred with monotonous regularity. But they had all learned to suffer in silence.

Then, when at last they had all begun to hope that they really must be approaching the end of the winter, an entirely new threat emerged. The Warden was taken ill and removed to hospital. Ginger Cat disappeared at the same time – presumably to a well-wisher. The Lodge fell empty and there was no longer any restriction to human access to the Nature Reserve. When the fact became known to the local human population, it was not long before gangs of boys with skates and toboggans were invading the Park, shattering its peace and quiet and destroying the freedom of its inhabitants. But, worse still, at night came poachers.

The first sounds of a gun came late one evening when Fox and Vixen were on the prowl. They stopped dead in their tracks, heads up sniffing the air, ears cocked for every slight sound.

'It can't be,' muttered Fox, looking at his mate. They waited. Then another bang convinced them of their suspicions and they dived for cover.

Under some shrubbery they listened with racing hearts, their bellies pressed to the frozen ground. They were a long way from their earth. As each second passed their nerves quivered in trepidation. There were no more shots, but then they saw two dark figures moving like shadows across the snow, not twenty yards from where they lay. Instinctively their heads went down in an attempt to render themselves even less conspicuous. But they could see what the figures were carrying and at the sight of it they both gasped.

'A deer!' they both hissed under their breath.

'And a large one, too,' said Fox, watching how the men were bent beneath its weight. 'Poor creature.'

'Is there nothing these humans won't stoop to?' Vixen said furiously. 'They know the very purpose of this Park is to preserve wildlife.'

'More to the point,' Fox reminded her, 'it was created a Nature Reserve to protect the very White Deer herd they are attacking.'

'Oh, where can our Warden have gone?' Vixen wailed.

'That we shan't know,' Fox said. 'But it is enough to know he is absent, and we are all unprotected.'

'The deer must be in a panic,' said Vixen. 'They've no experience of guns or of being hunted. And why *are* they hunted?'

'They're rare animals. Who knows what value the skin might have to a human who possesses one?'

'Then can *we* take that as some consolation? If the humans are only hunting the deer, maybe the other creatures here are not at risk.'

Fox laughed hollowly. 'It is my experience of such humans that all creatures are at risk as long as they have a gun in their hands.'

'Will they be back, do you think?' Vixen asked.

'As long as they know there is no Warden around, I think we can expect them,' Fox replied grimly.

His words were proved right. Although no guns were heard the next night, on the ensuing one they returned. The deer herd was frantic. Unlike their cousins in the unprotected wild and rugged areas of the country, they had nowhere to run to; no means of escape. What had been a haven of peace to them had now become a death-trap.

The other animals of the Park, who had always enjoyed a security from human intervention which was owed principally to the existence of the White Deer herd, forgot any obligation they should have felt. They only counted themselves lucky not to be the hunted ones. But the animals of Farthing Wood – the newcomers – were of a different mettle. From many different loyalties in their old home they had forged themselves into a unit

on their long march across country. They had learnt
during that period that the good of the individual usually
meant the good of the majority. The Park was now their
home, as it was the deer's, and they all of them felt some
responsibility towards their fellow inhabitants in fighting
their common enemy. But none of them could think of
anything they could do to prevent the poaching.

Fox and Vixen were again out foraging when the next
visit of the men with guns took place. This time they
were in a position to see everything. The deer herd were,
as usual, in the open part of the Park. In the absence of
the Warden they had lost their supplies of hay, and were
now reduced to digging beneath the snow with their
hooves as best they could to reach the grass and mosses
underneath. From the cover of a nearby clump of trees,
two men were creeping stealthily towards them.

The noble figure of the Great Stag himself towered
over the other deer, making a clear target for the guns.
Fox saw the men raising their weapons to take aim.
Without thinking, he commenced barking with an
abruptness that startled the already nervous deer. They
began to mill about, sensing danger again. When Vixen
joined in, Fox started to run towards the deer barking
as he went. He hoped the deer would take alarm and
run. The trick paid off. The more nervous of the deer
bolted, which alarmed the rest and they were soon run-
ning in all directions. Even the Great Stag ran, with a
backward glance at Fox over his shoulder. But, although
Fox may have saved the overlord of the Park, which had
been his main thought, he unconsciously hastened the
end of another. Unfortunately some of the deer ran
straight towards the trees where the men were hidden,
and so on to their guns. One was shot as they ap-
proached, causing the others to veer away. Then the
whole herd raced in panic as far as they could go, away

from the noise. But the men were satisfied with their stalking, and another white deer was removed from the Reserve.

'I hope my motives won't be misunderstood,' Fox said ruefully to Vixen. 'It might have looked as if I was in league with the killers.'

'Nonsense!' said Vixen. 'Is that likely? You aren't a man's pet but a creature of the Wild. You saved the Great Stag and he knows it.'

'But they still had their taste of blood. The herd is yet one fewer in number.'

'What can we do against the intelligence of humans?' Vixen asked. 'If they decided to slaughter every creature in the Park we could do nothing to stop it.'

'I'm not so pessimistic,' Fox said. 'All we have to do is to think of a way of preventing them getting into the Reserve.'

'Utterly impossible,' she replied flatly. 'How could we achieve that?'

'I don't know. Perhaps we could, at least, arrange a warning system at their approach so that we're not to be found when the men arrive.'

'And what would you do with the deer herd? Take them all underground?'

'All right,' Fox said wistfully. 'I suppose it's just wishful thinking, but there must be something that can be done to make them less vulnerable.'

'Oh, I know you when you're in this mood.' Vixen looked at him, and her great affection shone out of her eyes. 'You won't rest now. But thinking for a party of small animals that can hide themselves away is a far cry from causing a herd of deer to vanish.'

'I think I'll go and have a talk with the Great Stag,' Fox replied.

'I'll leave you then,' said Vixen. 'You won't want me around.'

'You couldn't be more wrong, my beloved Vixen,' he told her. 'I need you with me. You are my partner in everything.'

The Great Stag had not run far. He had been trying to muster the herd together again after the alarm. 'I am indebted to you,' he said to Fox at once. 'We only lost one. There was no scent of Man. We could have lost more.' He did not have the conceit to own that it was he who had been the prime target.

'We have to devise a way of preventing any more deaths,' Fox said earnestly.

'I spend all my waking hours trying to do so,' said the Stag. 'The fact is, without our supply of hay we may lose more animals from starvation than from the gun.'

'I can see it must be very difficult for the older and weaker among your herd to cope,' Fox agreed. 'But I am convinced we've seen the worst of the winter. The threat from Man, in my opinion, is far more severe.'

'You talk wisely,' said the Stag. 'I know you to be the intelligent animal who brought your friends here last summer from a great distance. But you didn't have large animals like us to contend with. I'm afraid the problem of ensuring our safety is well-nigh impossible.'

'You are repeating almost word for word what I've said to Fox,' Vixen remarked. 'Although our hearts are with you I don't believe we have the power to be of assistance.'

The Great Stag shook his noble head. 'If the Warden does not return I have decided there is only one course of action open to us.'

'I think I know what's in your mind,' said Fox quietly, 'for it has occurred to me also.'

'I fear we must leave the Park,' the Great Stag pronounced.

'Yes. It's as I expected. But outside you would run the same risk.'

'However, we could scatter over a wider area.'

Fox was silent for some moments. 'No,' he said finally in the determined manner that Vixen knew so well. 'It mustn't come to that. I won't admit defeat. I have the germ of an idea. Will you give me a day or so?'

'My dear friend,' the Stag said feelingly, 'you are under no obligation to do anything. You have your own problems. Of course I will give you whatever time you wish. I had not planned to leave our home just yet.'

'The men don't return every night,' Vixen said. 'You should be safe for the time being.'

Fox was deep in thought. 'I need to work things out,' he said presently. He turned to the Stag. 'We'll leave you now,' he said, 'and I will return to put my plan before you.'

'You are a gracious and clever animal,' replied the overlord of the Reserve. 'I shall await your coming again with the utmost eagerness.'

As Fox and Vixen turned after their farewells, she questioned him. 'May I ask what you have in mind?'

'I'll tell you all eventually,' he replied. 'It's the Pond, you see – that's the key to the whole thing.'

——15——
The Trap

The following afternoon the Park was invaded again by groups of young boys, most of them muffled to the chin to beat the cold, who had come to skate. The home of the Edible Frogs had been frozen over for months, but there were signs that a slight rise in temperature had occurred. In a few places the surface of the Pond had a little water on top of the ice. The youngsters, however, after inspecting thoroughly, donned their skates and proceeded to enjoy them selves.

From a snow-festooned bed of rushes Fox was watching their antics closely. He chuckled to himself as he thought of the many times Adder had waited at the waterside during the summer, patiently watching the

Edible Frogs disporting themselves. But his vigil was for a very different reason.

After an hour or so he had seen all he wanted to. Carefully avoiding any risk of being spotted by pairs of sharp young eyes, he made his way back to his earth. Vixen woke as he entered. She looked at him searchingly. 'Nothing yet,' was his only remark.

During the next couple of days the weather became noticeably milder, and for longer stretches the sun broke through the cloud formation that had loured upon the Park for so long. Each day Fox watched at the pond-side. On the second night the men returned and another deer was shot. The Great Stag in this time had not seen Fox again. Once more he began to think in terms of leaving the reserve.

But the very next afternoon Fox saw what he had been waiting for. The children arrived, but found their skating restricted. Almost a third of the Pond now had to be avoided, and they soon left it altogether in favour of tobogganing. Fox knew it was time for him to re-visit the Stag.

The great beast listened silently while he unfolded his plan, then raised his head and bellowed a challenge to the air, 'Now let them come,' he roared. Fox waited no longer. There was much to do.

But first he wanted Vixen's approval. During the journey to the Park he had relied a good deal on her judgement and had learnt to value it. She heard his plan and looked at him in admiration. Her enthusiasm did not need to be expressed in words. The Fox gathered all his friends together and put them in the picture also. They were totally in agreement save, predictably, for Tawny Owl who only gave grudging support.

'Can't see why you want to bother so much with a

deer herd,' he muttered. 'As long as the humans are banging away at them, *we're* that much safer.'

'But safer still if they can't "bang away" at *anything*' Fox said coolly.

'Very well,' said Badger. 'Now we must arrange for the sentries.'

So a system was arranged by which the animals were to watch the place where the poachers entered, the boundary between the Park and the road, and give early warning of their approach. Tawny Owl, Kestrel and Whistler were stationed at intervals along the fence. Along the ground Weasel, Hare, Badger and Vixen waited. Midway between the boundary and the Pond, Fox was stationed, while in the region of the Pond itself the Great Stag was patrolling in readiness to play his part in the Plan.

The first night passed without event, and at dawn the animals and birds returned to their homes. On the second night they were back at their posts. Although it was still cold, there was no longer the viciousness in the wind that had cut through their fur and feathers like a knife-blade. The snow that had covered the ground for so long had softened and, on the road outside the Park, had been churned into slush by motor vehicles. It was the noise of the steady squelch of steps through this slush that was the first sign to the waiting animals of the men's approach.

Weasel's sharp ears were the first to detect the sound. His small body, so close to the ground, had not the stature to see into the road. He ran quickly to the fence-post on which sat Tawny Owl. 'I hear footsteps!' he cried. 'Is it them?'

'I can see something coming,' replied Owl. 'Wait – yes, two figures . . . Yes! Yes! Quickly! Tell the others! I'm off to Fox!' He flew up in a wide arc over the treetops and sped off in the direction of the waiting Fox. Weasel passed the word to the others and together they raced back through the Park. Fox saw Tawny Owl approaching him at speed and himself prepared to run.

'To the Pond!' cried Owl. 'They're on their way!'

At once Fox set off at a breakneck pace, his breath coming like small bursts of steam from his mouth. Whistler and Kestrel were first back to safety. Vixen, Weasel and Badger had a long run ahead of them to keep in front of the men. Only Hare was almost as swift overland as the birds through the air.

Fox had told them to hide themselves once he had received the message. Out of sight they were quite safe from the poachers' guns. The men had come for larger game. But it was not in the nature of the animals of Farthing Wood to disassociate themselves from such an important event – and one in which the leader was placing himself in danger. So the slower animals had condemned themselves to run across an exhausting stretch of parkland to be in on things. Of the three Vixen was by far the fastest and she outdistanced Weasel and Badger as quickly as Hare had outdistanced her. Weasel, although far smaller than Badger, was much more lithe and had a far more elastic and rippling running pace. But he moderated his speed to suit the older animal's comfort.

As his friends hastened back to join him, Fox was on his way to join the Stag. The scion of the deer herd had agreed to keep his station by the Pond each night until he saw Fox again. He lowered his head as he saw the familiar chestnut body racing towards him.

'Hold – yourself – ready,' gasped Fox, his tongue lolling painfully from his mouth. 'They're coming.'

'So tonight is to be the night,' the Stag intoned. 'Rest

awhile, my friend. You appear to be somewhat distressed.'

'No, I – mustn't stop – I must complete the – task,' Fox panted. 'I – have to make – sure they – find you.' And he was off again, back in the direction from which he had come – back towards the men with guns. He passed a black poplar in whose boughs clustered Tawny Owl, Kestrel and Whistler. But they did not interrupt him and he did not see them. He did see Hare but there was no time to stop and he went by without a glance. Next he passed Vixen who gave him a longing look. He half looked back as he ran, but even she had to be ignored for the sake of the Plan. When he spotted Badger and Weasel in the distance he dropped on all fours, for behind them the two fateful shadows were approaching.

'Go to cover,' he told his friends as they reached him. 'No need to endanger more of us than necessary.' They passed on and Fox waited to begin the gamble of his life.

Among the snow-coated sedges by the Pond lay Hare. He was watching the White Stag nervously tossing his head as he stood by the edge of the ice, his legs quivering. Vixen found him and lay down. She was unable to speak. Her heart was pounding unmercifully. Eventually Badger and Weasel tottered in to join them. There they waited and watched.

Twenty yards from the men, Fox stood up and yapped loudly. The signal was heard and out from the nearby copse came the White Deer herd, slowly, timidly, in knots of three and four. The men stopped. One pointed and their voices made themselves heard. They were looking among the herd and Fox knew who they were looking for. But the one they wanted was missing. The human voices were heard again – harsh, rough voices. The deer paused. Fox yapped again and started towards them. The deer scattered as instructed, running in the direction of the Pond. The men shouted angrily, now pointing at the fox. This was the animal that had frustrated them before. Fox ran behind the herd as if driving them. His back was to the men, and every nerve-end along his neck, his spine and his haunches was strung as taut as a guitar string. The hackles rose on his coat for he knew he was courting death. At last he had to glance back. He saw one of the men raise his gun. It was aimed at him, the cause of their wrath. But Fox had no intention of being shot. He wheeled away at a right-angle, running fast, then twisted and swerved, twisted and swerved, like a hare followed by hounds. A shot rang out but the bullet found no mark.

Now the men were running, for their quarry was escaping. They would have one deer, if not the one they were after. The herd reached the brink of the Pond and spread out, screening its edge. In front of them, on to the ice itself, stepped the Great Stag. Cautiously he went, pausing at each step, until he reached the limit of safety. As the men came up, the herd swung away to the right, leaving the Stag exposed – solitary, undefended, alone on the ice. The men saw their passage was clear on the left side of the Pond. The Stag's head was turned away as if he were ignorant of their intention. They edged out, foot by foot, on the treacherous ice. They meant to have him this time. At the moment they raised their weapons Fox barked a third time. The Stag swung his great head round, saw the men and, with a tremendous bound leapt for the shore. But the poachers were committed now. They saw their target about to escape from their grip again. They ran forward to take aim at the retreating animal and then – crash! suddenly it was as if their feet were snatched from under them, and they were plunging down, down into black, icy water. Their guns were thrown away as they sought to save themselves, floundering and trying to find a handhold on something.

The Great Stag turned at the edge of the ice and saw the weapons meant for his death sink to the murky depths of the Pond's bottom, abandoned without a thought by their owners. At this clear evidence that Fox's plan had worked to perfection the Stag laid his head back and bellowed in triumph. Then Fox was surrounded by his jubilant friends – his old friends and the whole of the deer herd. The Great Stag joined them. 'That,' he boomed, 'is a piece of animal cunning never likely to be surpassed.'

While the animals were milling around, the men were striking out for the shore. The Pond was not deep and they were in no danger save that of a severe ducking and a bad chill. Their cries of anger had changed to cries of distress before they had pulled their frozen, dripping bodies clear of the water on to the shore. They cast one look at the bevy of wild creatures who had bested them, and then set off at an uncomfortable trot. Their misery would not be over for a while, for back they had to go across the Park and along the slushy road before there was any hope of being dry and warm again. At every step the icy coldness of their drenched clothing chafed at their bodies and neither of them could imagine a discomfort existed that could be more severe.

'I think we've seen the last of them,' said Hare. 'Fox, this is your greatest day. Even on our long journey you never reached these heights.'

Fox felt the admiration of all the creatures swell like a tide around him, but he was content to know that his plan had worked without mishap. Only Vixen, in all her fierce pride, felt a nagging doubt about what might be the reaction of two humans degraded and humiliated beyond belief by a fox.

16
One Good Turn...

Fox's courage and ingenuity were now the byword of the inhabitants of White Deer Park. It was no new discovery for his old friends from Farthing Wood, but he was the acknowledged hero of the deer herd, and even those creatures who had not been witness to the events at the Pond heard the story and marvelled. Once again he was brimful of confidence after his successes with the chickens and now the poachers. In both instances he had pitted his wits against humans and each time emerged triumphant.

So Fox had a special status in the Reserve and, although still underweight from the rigours of the winter, he carried his head more erect, his gait was looser and the sparkle had returned to his eyes. Vixen was delighted. 'You're your old self again,' she told him. Yet still that unnameable thought lurked in her mind.

For the next few weeks the weather fluctuated. Warm spells were followed by cold spells which then gave way to milder temperatures again. Most of the old snow had melted, but there were still heavy frosts at night and new, but slighter, falls of snow still occurred. But the Park no longer seemed to be deserted. The inhabitants were out and about again when it was safe, and all sensed the coming of Spring. Food was easier to find for all creatures and health and appearance improved.

One day in late February Whistler found Squirrel, Vole and Fieldmouse enjoying together some nuts which Squirrel had been able to dig up from the softer ground.

'I don't think you need me any more, do you?' he asked, referring to the trips the birds were still making to the general store's dump.

'Not really,' replied Squirrel. 'But we're most grateful. You may have kept us alive.'

'It's not quite Spring yet,' Vole pointed out, shaking his head. 'I wouldn't like to say for sure – '

'Nonsense,' cut in the more reasonable Fieldmouse. 'Whistler and Kestrel – and Tawny Owl too – have done more than enough for us. It's time they had a rest.'

Vole was outnumbered and conceded defeat. 'At any rate,' he persisted, 'if things should get difficult again I imagine we can still call on you?'

Whistler bowed elaborately and winked at the other two animals. 'Always at your service,' he answered with a hint of sarcasm. 'I'll tell Kestrel the news.'

The hawk had been on a similar errand to Rabbit and Hare. 'So we've both been released?' he said as Whistler concurred.

'I can't say I'm sorry,' Whistler admitted. 'The job

was definitely acquiring a considerable degree of tedium.'

'Well, I think we can say no-one ever heard a word of complaint from us,' Kestrel remarked. 'Though the same couldn't be said of Owl. His constant grumbling is enough to wear you down. Some days I simply can't bring myself to talk to him.'

'Oh, it's only his way,' laughed the good-natured heron. 'His heart's in the right place really.'

'D'you think so? I sometimes wonder. But I suppose you're right.' Kestrel gave Whistler a mischievous glance. 'Er – have you told Tawny Owl yet?' he asked.

'No,' replied Whistler. 'I suppose we'd better go and –' He broke off as he noticed Kestrel's expression. 'Are you thinking what I think you're thinking, Kestrel?'

Kestrel screeched with laughter. 'Undoubtedly,' he said.

'Well, I don't know. . . .' Whistler said hesitantly.

'Pah! Teach him a lesson!' Kestrel said shortly. 'He won't know we've stopped because he sleeps during the day.'

Whistler reluctantly agreed. He was not one for perpetrating jokes on others. 'But we mustn't let him continue for long,' he insisted.

So poor Tawny Owl carried on flying outside the Park at night to fetch what he could from the usual spot. The animals the food was destined for said nothing as they never saw him arrive with it, and assumed all the birds had changed their minds. Then one night, as he was flying over the road, Tawny Owl saw two figures which he thought he recognized. He paused with his load on a nearby bough to make sure. He did not need long to ascertain that it was the two poachers abroad again and seemingly on their way to the Park. He watched them long enough to see that they appeared to be unarmed, but decided to fly straight to Fox to warn him of their approach.

On his way he saw Badger ambling along. 'Good gracious!' Badger called up, seeing the bird with his load. 'Are you still doing that, Owl?'

Tawny Owl dropped what he was carrying at once and landed by Badger. '*What* did you say?' he demanded.

Badger unfortunately began to laugh. 'I think you've been the victim of someone's joke,' he chuckled. 'The other birds stopped flying to the dump days ago.'

Tawny Owl's beak dropped open. Then he snorted angrily. 'So that's it,' he said. 'That's how I'm treated for trying to help others.'

'Oh dear,' Badger muttered to himself. He thought quickly. 'No, no,' he said, 'they just forgot to tell you, I expect. Er – don't take it amiss,' he added hastily.

But Tawny Owl was in high dudgeon. He stalked round and round Badger, rustling his wings furiously and a hard glint came into his huge eyes. 'So they forgot, did they?' he hissed. 'We'll see how much forgetting *I* can do, then.' His last words were uttered with a menace that alarmed Badger, though he did not know that Tawny Owl was referring to the warning he had meant to bring. Then the bird flew off, climbing higher and higher in the sky until he was far away from any of his companions.

'Oh dear, oh dear,' wailed Badger. 'He's really angry now. I wish I hadn't laughed. Whatever did he mean by his last remark? I shall never know now, and it might have been important.'

'And after all,' he thought to himself as he trotted homeward, 'it wasn't a very nice trick. He *was* doing it for others. I wonder who's behind it?' He made his way to Fox's earth but Fox and Vixen were missing. Badger decided to wait.

When his friends eventually returned, Badger told them of Tawny Owl's feelings. Fox shook his head. 'He hates being made a fool of,' he said. 'He won't forget this for a long time. He's a very proud bird – and I think he's sensitive too, underneath. We've not been very kind to him.'

'*I* didn't know he was still collecting food,' Badger said.

'Neither did we,' said Vixen. 'It must be Kestrel's idea. He and Tawny Owl don't always see eye to eye.'

'But he'll be blaming *all* of us,' Fox said. 'He'll feel we've ganged up on him. I know him.'

'What can we do?' Badger asked. 'He flew a long way off. We may not see him for days.'

'Kestrel must apologise,' Fox said firmly. 'I shall tell him so.'

'Poor old Owl,' said kindly Vixen. 'It's not fair.'

As they conversed, none of them was aware that the poachers had entered the Park once again. It was Weasel who saw them approaching, but he stayed to watch. He knew where their guns lay and thought the men no longer posed a threat.

They seemed to be searching for *something* though, Weasel was sure, it could not be for the White Deer. He followed them, and was relieved to see they were going away from his and his friends' area of the Park. Suddenly one of the men nudged his companion and pointed. An animal was trotting briskly over the snowy patches only some ten yards away. Weasel could see plainly it was a fox. He knew it was not his fox because of the gait. Both men had pulled pistols from their pockets. One of them fired immediately at the animal but missed. The fox stopped in its tracks and, for a second, glanced back. It saw the men and started to run. But it was not quick enough. Another shot, this time from the other pistol, brought it down.

Weasel, keeping well out of sight and with a fiercely pounding heart, saw the men walk over to the stricken creature and examine it. One of them put a boot under its body and turned it over. It was quite dead. But the men were not satisfied. They did not turn back as if intending to leave the Park, but continued on their way in the same furtive, searching manner. Weasel followed them no longer. He needed to see no more to recognize the men's purpose. It was imperative to find Fox and Vixen.

Luckily the two distant cracks of the pistols had been heard by them and Badger, and they were debating what the new sounds of guns could mean when the breathless Weasel found them.

'It's the same two men,' he told them. 'But they're not after deer. They've got small guns and they've just shot a fox.'

Fox and Vixen both gulped nervously.

'You *must* take cover underground,' Weasel went on. 'They – ' he broke off as another shot was heard. The four animals looked at each other in horror.

'They're after all the foxes,' whispered Vixen. 'I dreaded this.'

'No,' said Fox grimly. 'They're after me. It's revenge they want for the trick I played them. They'll kill every fox they can in the hope that one of them will be me.'

Weasel nodded miserably. 'That's exactly the conclusion I came to,' he said. 'Please, Fox, take shelter.'

With a dazed expression, Fox allowed himself to be led to his earth where he numbly followed Vixen underground.

'We'd better make ourselves scarce, too,' Weasel said to Badger. 'We must have been seen at the pond-side along with Fox. We can't be too careful.'

In his den Fox was shaking his head and muttering, 'What have I done? What have I done?'

'You did what you thought best,' Vixen soothed him. 'And it was a brilliant plan.'

'But what have I achieved?' Fox demanded. 'I've set our enemies more firmly against us. The deer might be saved – they can't shoot *them* with pistols – but now I've brought even greater danger to *us*.'

'You weren't to know this would happen,' she assured him. 'You acted with the best intentions.'

Fox stood up. 'But how can I skulk around here while innocent creatures are being shot?' he cried. 'It's *me* they want. How many other foxes have to die while I hide away? I'm putting every other fox in the Park at risk.'

'And what do you intend to do?' Vixen asked angrily. 'Run up to the humans and offer yourself as a sacrifice?'

'At least if they killed me they would be satisfied. Then the Park *would* be safe again.'

'Don't talk such foolishness, Fox,' Vixen said in desperation, seeing the look on his face. 'Will they recognize you as the fox who made fools of them? To a human we all look the same. You would be killed and still they would hunt for others.'

'Then they *will* kill every fox,' he said. 'Only in that way can they be sure they have got rid of me.'

'Is it likely with the sounds of guns again, that any wild creature will stay abroad? By now they'll all be lying low,' Vixen said.

Fox looked at her and marvelled. '*You* are the wise one, dear Vixen,' he said, 'not I.'

'Pooh, you're merely blinded by your concern,' she replied.

'But what can I do?' he moaned.

Vixen knew how to handle her mate. 'You devised a

plan before. Now you must use your wits again,' she said. 'It's your brain that's our safety measure.'

Fox smiled and was already calmer as he settled down to think. 'Whatever did I do before we met?' he murmured. 'My brave counsellor.'

——17——
...Deserves Another

Tawny Owl, feeling very aggrieved, had flown as far away from his friends in the Park as he could without actually flying over its boundaries. His pride was hurt and, as he moodily munched his supper, his indignation grew with every mouthful.

'Serves them right if they never see me again,' he muttered. 'And a fat lot they'd care if they didn't.' He went and hunched himself up on a sycamore branch and brooded. With each minute he felt more and more unwanted. He had done the worst possible thing for himself by disassociating from all those he knew. For, on his own, he had nothing to do but brood over his misery; whereas in company a cheery word or two from someone would have made him forget his hurts far more quickly.

However, in his own company, he had no appearances to keep up; no risk of losing face. He began to wonder after a while if he had over-reacted. He sat and thought.

It was probably not true that all the animals had collaborated to make him look a fool. Fox, he was sure, would never be a party to such a thing. And neither would Badger, although he had chuckled at his discomfiture. The more he thought of Fox, of whom he was genuinely fond, the more guilty he felt. To what fate might he have consigned Fox and Vixen by not warning them of the return of the poachers? They surely had been on the way to the Park, and who could say for what purpose? He shifted about on the branch, feeling more and more uncomfortable and nervous. If anything had happened, he could never forgive himself. In the end he could stay put no longer. He leapt from the bough and sallied forth in the direction in which he had first spotted the men.

The darkness was fading as he flew over the Park, and he spied the poachers in the act of clambering back through the fence before they jumped the ditch. He was glad they were leaving, but was fearful of what they might have left behind them. A little further on he saw something that made his stomach turn over. The body of a fox lay crumpled on the snow, its red blood mingling with the white ground. Tawny Owl, of course, immediately thought the worst. He had murdered Fox. He fluttered to a tree and sank down, overcome by weakness. Drained of all feeling, he contemplated his own selfishness. It was a long time before he could force himself to approach the body. At length, with a heavy heart and wings of lead, he managed to fly over to it.

As he came close he knew it was not Fox; neither was it Vixen. His spirits lifted, but only for a few brief minutes. Because, not very much further away, a second fox corpse greeted his sight. This time he examined it at once. A second time he was relieved. But now he wondered how many deaths had occurred. Was his friend lying dead somewhere after all? He flew off again, combing the ground afresh as he went. He went this way and that, and then back again, frantically searching the Reserve yard by yard for the sight he dreaded to see. None of the night creatures watched Tawny Owl's agony. For a long time they had been in refuge. But as the sun came up, Tawny Owl dropped with exhaustion. And there – high, high up in the glittering blue of the winter sky Kestrel soared, and saw him fall.

Later in the day Mole, whose joy in tunnelling had been unindulged while the ground had been at its hardest, now found his freedom restored. Where the snow had melted the ground was very soft once any overnight frost had disappeared. Mole had made a new shaft that ran up to the surface, and was poking his head into the open, his pink snout quivering excitedly. As it happened he was almost squashed by a hoof of the Great Stag who was walking that way.

The giant animal looked down at the tiny velvet-clad body beneath him. 'I beg your pardon,' he said. 'I didn't see you at first. I'm looking for your friend Fox. I understand the humans returned to the Park last night.'

'Yes, Badger told me of it,' replied Mole. 'We all thought we'd seen the last of them.'

'Your leader is very brave and doesn't always think of himself. It appears that he may have piled up some trouble for his efforts the other night. It is now our turn to assist him. Hence the reason for my visit.'

Mole gave the Stag directions to Fox's earth, and went to tell Badger of his encounter.

Fox and Vixen were not in their den. They were out foraging, for it had now become unsafe to leave shelter at night. So the Great Stag, having assured himself of their absence, passed the time by grazing where he could until they should return. Eventually he saw them coming as he chewed a mouthful of moss.

'Greetings,' he said simply. 'I've come to inform you that the entire deer herd is at your disposal if you need us in your *new* dispute with the human killers.'

Fox listened to the Stag's gentle tone of irony. 'I fear there's nothing new about it,' he replied. 'I have always looked upon them as our enemies as well as yours.'

'Have you decided on any course of action should they return again?'

'Oh, they'll be back,' Fox said. 'I hardly think they'll be satisfied with their work so far. Kestrel tells me there are two dead foxes. The men must know there are many more than that still living.'

'My advice would be for us to stay under cover every night until they decide to come no more,' said Vixen, 'but Fox won't listen.'

'Simply because we have no way of knowing their intentions,' he explained. 'How long would it be before they came looking for us in our earths? Then there *would* be no escape.'

'You have a plan then?' the Stag asked.

'Only a poor one, I'm afraid. But it may work.'

'I am all ears.'

'To be honest,' began Fox, 'it isn't really a plan at all. I've merely been thinking along the lines of finding the safest spot in the Park and then going there. It occurred to me that there is one place these poaching humans might perhaps not care to venture to, and that is the grounds of the Warden's own garden, around the Lodge. If we holed up in there we might avoid them.'

'Hm,' the Stag murmured, considering. 'And what of the other foxes in the Reserve?'

'My immediate concern, naturally, is for my mate and my friends,' Fox said. 'But it would, no doubt, be possible to pass the word to them, in case they should feel like joining us.'

'I can foresee problems,' the Stag commented. 'These other foxes haven't the same feelings for your friends as you have. I should imagine they would look upon the presence of your mouse and rabbit friends as a ready-made food supply.'

'There would be no need for the voles and fieldmice to leave their homes,' answered Fox. 'The humans are not interested in small fry like them. But it's true; the question of the rabbits needs some thought.'

'Well, I have an idea that might make yours unnecessary,' the Great Stag told him, 'if you are willing to go along with it. It is perfectly simple. If the humans return, and appear to be bent on killing again, I have orders for the whole of my herd to charge them *en masse*. With that sort of force arraigned against them, I don't think they will need a lot of persuading to leave.'

'What if they use their pistols on the deer?' asked Fox.

'We're quite prepared for the possibility,' answered the Stag. 'But it's a risk we must take. We feel it is time we repaid your good turn to us. In any case, I honestly doubt if these wretched humans will stand still long enough when they see us all thundering towards them. There will be more than a few pairs of lowered antlers for them to negotiate.'

Fox and Vixen could not help but chuckle as they pictured the scene. 'I think it's an admirable and very generous idea,' said Vixen.

'It's certainly that,' agreed Fox. 'The only thing that comes into my mind is, that it could only work once. If

they are still determined to enter the Park after that,
they would make sure of the herd's whereabouts first.
You can't cover every corner.'

'Then we must make sure our charge is so terrifying
that they are dissuaded for good from coming back,' the
Stag said. 'Are you willing to give it a try?'

'Assuredly, yes.'

'Then I'll go to make preparations.'

'I will arrange for sentries along the perimeter as
before,' Fox said. He turned to Vixen. 'I wonder what
happened to Tawny Owl?'

Kestrel knew. He had found the exhausted owl on the
open ground, without even the strength to fly up into a
tree.

'I'm glad you've come back,' said the hawk, 'but sorry
to see you in this state.'

Tawny Owl slowly shook his head, too weak to reply.

'I have an apology to make,' Kestrel went on. 'At
Fox's insistence. I'm afraid I'm to blame for not telling
you to stop flying to the dump. It was a rotten trick and
I very much regret it.'

Tawny Owl blinked once or twice and nodded. 'All
– for – gotten,' he gasped.

'You need something to eat to restore your strength,'
said Kestrel. 'I'll see if I can – '

'No,' said Tawny Owl. 'Just rest.'

'But you can't stay on the ground – too vulnerable,'
insisted the hawk.

'Can't – fly. Too – weak,' came the reply.

'I see. Well, I'll keep a look-out until you've recovered
a bit.'

From the sky, where he floated effortlessly on air cur-
rents or hovered in his inimitable way, Kestrel could see

Mole, the Great Stag, Fox and Vixen. He wondered what was afoot. After checking once or twice on Tawny Owl's progress, he swooped down to speak to Fox.

'I've found Owl,' he said. 'Goodness knows where he's been. He's completely exhausted.'

'Where is he?' Fox asked. 'I need him tonight.'

'Don't know if he's much use at the moment,' said Kestrel. 'What's astir?'

Fox explained the Great Stag's idea.

'I understand,' said the hawk. 'I'll take you to Tawny Owl.'

The sight of Fox approaching him across the parkland was the best medicine for Tawny Owl that could have been produced. Now, at last, he knew his friend was safe. He tottered to his feet and stood, a little unsteadily.

'My dear Owl,' Fox said in great distress. 'Whatever has happened? You look dreadful.'

'It's all right – now,' said Tawny Owl. 'Thank heaven you're still alive, And Vixen too?'

'Yes. She's well.'

'I'm so glad. I saw the men last night – with guns. I meant to tell you, but – well, you know how I react when my pride takes a blow. I'm sure Badger has told you he saw me carrying the – er – well, you know,' he finished lamely.

'I understand perfectly,' said Fox. 'I won't question you any further. None of us will. But you must rest all you can. I shall need you as a look-out again tonight. Will you be able?'

'By then I shall have recovered,' Tawny Owl assured him. 'I think I can fly a little now. I'll go home and sleep properly. Where will you need me?'

'The same place as before. Our friends the deer are preparing a little reception committee.'

Tawny Owl nodded and, still bleary-eyed, took his leave.

'Kestrel,' said Fox. 'I'm relying on you to get the others to their places by the fence. They must be there by dusk.'

'Your wish,' answered Kestrel, 'is my command.'

'Very well,' said Fox. 'And tonight I, for once, shall stay firmly in the background.'

Sure enough, Fox's belief in the poachers' persistence in revenge was proved well-founded. This time they were spotted early on in the evening and the message was passed back along the lines to the Great Stag who quickly mustered his herd. It was then necessary for Fox, Vixen, Badger and Weasel to make themselves scarce before the advance of the men. Along with Hare and the birds, they decided to watch events from the Hollow from where, if necessary, they could make a quick escape to their homes.

The poachers seemed to be in a very ugly mood. Any sign of movement anywhere was enough to set them shooting and, at each report, the watching Farthing Wood animals shuddered at what might have been the fate of some unsuspecting night creature.

Foot by foot, the men entered further into the Park. Foot by foot they decreased the distance between themselves and the White Deer. The deer waited in some agitation. They disliked standing still as danger approached. Some cropped the grass nervously, while others tossed their heads and flicked their short tails. Only the Great Stag, at their head, stood impassive.

They saw the men getting closer from behind the line of trees that helped to screen them. The Great Stag's eyes narrowed as he waited for the right moment. The men remained ignorant. Then he threw his head back and roared like a stag in rut. The deer herd bounded through the trees and raced towards the poachers. The men looked up, startled, at the white mass that galloped towards them, their hooves thundering as in a stampede; a forest of antlers lowered in line. With shouts the men turned and began to run hell for leather back across the grassland. Neither paused a second to take aim. They could only run and run, as fast as they could, away from the white animal tide that threatened to engulf them. Fear lent wings to their feet, for otherwise they must have been caught.

As they neared the Park fence, the deer slackened their pace and swept round in a circle, back towards the open land where they usually stayed, the Great Stag still leading them. The men had gone.

From the Hollow came excited voices.

'Did it work? Have they gone?' asked Hare.

Tawny Owl flew to see. 'Yes, they've gone,' he reported.

'And this time for good,' said Badger.

'How are you so sure?' Weasel wanted to know. 'We all believed that last time.'

'Twice they've been defeated by animals,' said Badger. 'Are they prepared to risk a third tussle?'

'Only if,' said Tawny Owl slowly, 'they are sure they can win.'

Fox looked at him. 'Well,' he said, 'we still have my idea in reserve.'

—— **18** ——

Two Friends Return

All was quiet again in White Deer Park for some days. But in the last invasion by the poachers another of the Farthing Wood rabbits had lost its life – this time by the gun, for the men had shot indiscriminately. Fox felt this loss more deeply than any, for he knew that it was he that had, indirectly, caused the death of one of his friends. Rabbit had come to inform him of the death.

'Another one of our does gone,' he had said after explaining how he had found the body. 'And this Park was to be a haven for us! What sort of a haven is it when we rabbits have been thinned out to a mere remnant of those that lived in Farthing Wood?'

'I know, I know,' Fox answered miserably. 'I've had the same from Vole and Fieldmouse. It's very distressing. We couldn't have expected such a terrible winter – nor this other threat to our survival. The idea of a Nature Reserve is that it should be a sanctuary for all wildlife within. These murderous humans seem to have no respect even for their own laws.'

'Well, let's hope the winter has sent its worst,' rejoined Rabbit. 'But what can we expect from the humans?'

'Who knows?' Fox answered frankly. 'They may be back again. They may not. Shall we try and be optimistic about it?'

'I suppose it's all we *can* do,' agreed Rabbit.

'At any rate,' Fox said brightly, 'you rabbits will soon be back at your usual numbers, I'll warrant. Your powers of recovery, you know . . . .'

'Why is it the only thing we seem to be renowned for is how fast we breed?' Rabbit wanted to know. 'I bet we're no more prolific than the mice. But, you see, Fox, any danger that's around inhibits our desire to breed. You know how timid we are.'

'I do indeed,' Fox said. 'Never ever will I forget the river crossing.' He referred to an incident during the animals' long journey to the Park when the rabbits had panicked badly and caused a disaster.

'All right, all right,' nodded Rabbit. 'Neither am I ever likely to, even if allowed.'

'No hurt intended, I assure you,' said Fox quickly.

'Don't mention it,' was the reply. Then Rabbit smiled. 'Where else in the Wild would a fox talk so politely to a rabbit?'

Fox smiled back, and Rabbit turned to go.

The afternoon brought an excited Kestrel to Fox's earth. His piercing cries brought Fox and Vixen hurriedly to the surface.

'What is it, Kestrel? You *do* seem in a state,' Fox said.

'I've just spotted that ginger cat walking in the Warden's garden,' he shrieked.

Fox misunderstood the motive for the hawk's excitement. 'Calm down, calm down,' he said. 'You just make sure you don't go in too close, and he won't attack you again. Your scars healed perfectly, didn't they?'

'No, no, it's not that,' Kestrel said hurriedly. 'I hadn't even thought of it. You don't seem to have grasped the significance of the cat's reappearance. The Warden must be back!' He looked triumphantly at the pair of foxes, as if he had brought the man and his cat back personally.

'Of course!' said Fox. 'The cat disappeared at the same time, didn't he? Oh but, Kestrel, can we be sure?'

'I would have hovered around a little longer to *make* sure,' said Kestrel, 'but I wanted to bring you the news.'

'It's marvellous news,' said Vixen. 'It means we can all breathe again. The poachers won't dare come back now.'

'I'll fly straight back and see if I can spot our protector,' Kestrel offered. 'Then we can spread the word.'

'Oh, this calls for a celebration,' said Fox happily. 'If the Warden is indeed back with us our worries are over.'

The Warden *had* returned and, to prove it, was seen on his rounds later in the day by many of the animals. Badger and Fox stood together by Badger's set talking.

'What changes will he see since he went away?' Badger mused. 'If only we could tell him of those who have been killed.'

'If he counts the head of white deer he will see their numbers have dropped,' said Fox. 'But he may not be suspicious of it.'

'How I wish those slaughterers could be brought before him,' growled Badger. 'Why should they escape their punishment?'

'Well, we're helpless in the matter,' said Fox. 'But, at

least, no more creatures will meet their fate in the Park at *their* hands.'

Little did Fox imagine then that Badger's wish was to be fulfilled, and that the animals of Farthing Wood were to be the instruments of bringing the offenders to justice. For the poachers, ignorant of the Warden's return, were about to make one trip too many to the Nature Reserve.

Fox's own cunning, which perhaps led him to anticipate better than other creatures the way humans might behave, was to be proved right again in his doubts expressed to the Great Stag. The poachers, it seemed, were still determined to wreak revenge where they could, although they now knew they must avoid the deer herd. That very evening they entered the Park at a different point, intent on redressing the balance in their favour by the work of their pistols.

Relieved, as they thought, of the need to stay under cover at night, a lot of the animals, as well as Tawny Owl, were abroad at the time on their various errands. But, separated as they were, they all stopped in their tracks at the same instant as they heard once more the report of a gun.

Fox and Vixen were, as usual, together. 'I don't believe it,' Vixen whispered. 'They can't have come back again.'

'The noise came from that direction,' Fox indicated. 'We haven't heard it from there before.' He scowled. 'The murdering scoundrels,' he said thickly. 'Come on, Vixen, we'd better get back.'

But Vixen did not move.

'What's the matter?' Fox asked. 'We can't stay here.'

'Perhaps it would be better *not* to go back,' Vixen said cryptically.

Fox looked at her in astonishment.

'Do you recall your latest plan?' she reminded him.

'The Warden's garden?' he asked. 'But it's not necessary, now he's back. These men are *his* quarrel now.'

'Exactly,' replied his mate. 'And we can lead him to them – or rather *them* to him.'

'Phew!' gasped Fox. 'That's a little ambitious – even for us.'

'Yes, it is,' she acknowledged. 'But don't we all want these men caught? Well, we *could* make that more likely.'

Fox, as so often, looked at her in sheer admiration. 'You are a wonder,' he said. 'I'm sure we *could* do it. But we must be very, very careful.'

At the sound of the gun Tawny Owl had automatically played his part. He flew straight to where the shot had been fired to locate the danger. He saw the men and, this time, no victim. The shot had gone astray. Back in the direction of the home area he winged his way and, spying Fox and Vixen from the air, told them what he had found. Fox sent him to warn Badger, Weasel and any of the others around to exercise the utmost caution, and to tell them of Vixen's suggestion. Silently Tawny Owl flew off.

'I want to handle this myself,' Fox said to her. 'I don't want you at risk too.'

'I'll stay well clear,' she replied. 'But I'll be right behind you.'

Fox slunk off through the shadows to offer himself as bait to the poachers, while Vixen crept in his wake, twenty yards distant. The men were easily spotted, stirring up the dead undergrowth with sticks for any hapless creature cowering beneath. But Fox, safe behind a broad oak tree, yapped as he had yapped before in their hearing. The men looked up and saw a shadowy figure under the trees. At once they gave chase, both firing haphazardly. Fox, his body close to the ground, sped away through the copse towards the Warden's Lodge. Behind the men ran Vixen, nervous, frightened, but with every nerve tingling.

Tawny Owl had rounded up Badger, Hare, Weasel and Rabbit. Then he went on to inform the Great Stag and the deer herd. Together all these animals began to converge from different directions on the focal point. No-one wanted to be left out of the adventure, and Rabbit had a particular wish to see himself avenged. The lights were on in the cottage, for the Warden also had heard the gunfire and was preparing to investigate. Badger even spotted Ginger Cat roaming outside the door. All seemed to be set for the finale.

Fox ran swiftly on a looping course for the cottage lights, making himself moderate his speed to keep the men within distance of him. As he neared his goal, he saw the Warden framed in the doorway and, to the left of the Lodge, the deer herd milling about in spectral array. Too late the poachers saw where they were running and stopped. As they tried to swing away to run from their fate, the deer herd rushed towards them, surrounding them, and buffeted them off their feet. The Warden raced over and shouted back towards his open door. While Fox and Vixen delightedly mingled with their watching friends a second man, whom Badger recognized as the animal doctor, ran out of the house. The poachers were collared and marched indoors. For a moment, in the doorway, the Warden turned back. He looked at the array of wild creatures strangely gathered together before his home. Each one of them looked towards him, and an expression came over his face of a wonderful compassion and affection that lit an answering flame in their own hearts. The moment passed, but there was a timelessness about it that was never to be forgotten. When he had gone, the most complete and utter silence reigned.

Finally the Great Stag spoke, rather stumblingly and inadequately. He was greatly moved. 'My friends, today we have formed a new bond of companionship,' he said. 'Today we are at one with Nature – er – and humanity.'

No-one else spoke or moved. The air above, the ground beneath were shot with magic; a strange echo of an Ancient World that none of them could comprehend had sounded in White Deer Park.

—19—
Thaw

The spell was broken by the movement of Ginger Cat who walked nonchalantly over to Badger. He seemed quite undeterred by the memory of their fight.

'We meet again,' he purred enigmatically.

Badger nodded. 'I hope in happier circumstances?' he ventured.

'Certainly,' came the reply. 'I'm quite aware I owe my life to your forbearance. Er – how is your friend the hawk?'

'Perfectly well,' answered Badger. 'And yourself?'

'Oh, couldn't be better,' the cat said. 'But I must say I'm relieved to be back here. I was taken to a spot miles away and shut up with a lot of other cats in cages while my mast – ah, I mean the man, was treated for his illness.'

Badger smiled at the cat's slip of the tongue, and Ginger Cat smiled back. He and Badger knew each other pretty well.

Fox and Vixen came over for a word, and the Great Stag led the deer herd away.

'Well, you all look a lot happier since I saw you last,' said Ginger Cat. 'And I'm glad to see, Fox, you've put on a little weight.'

'Oh yes,' said Fox. 'We've had some hard times, but we've come through all right.'

Badger recalled Toad's last words before hibernation when he had wished they would all 'come through' the winter. How long ago that seemed. And now, with the temperature steadily rising, they could all look forward to their friend's re-appearance. But, of course, they had not all 'come through'. What changes Toad would see in their numbers.

'You seem very pensive, Badger,' remarked Ginger Cat. 'What is it?'

'Oh, nothing really,' he said. 'Just thinking of old friends.'

Weasel, Tawny Owl, Hare and Rabbit joined them.

'Three times we've overcome those humans,' Rabbit said proudly. 'They must think the Park is jinxed.'

'The ones we've just seen caught?' Ginger Cat enquired. 'What happened before? You must tell me your news.'

'I will,' Badger offered. 'But another time, my feline friend. It's been quite a night.'

Hare felt inclined to mention to his cousin Rabbit that he had not seen *him* much in evidence on the two previous occasions, but decided against it. It was not a time for needless criticism.

The animals and Tawny Owl bid Ginger Cat farewell and, together, wandered slowly away from the cottage.

'I think we're entitled to have that celebration now,' Vixen said to her mate.

'Yes, I think so too. Now, truly, our troubles are over.'

'But our party is incomplete,' said Badger. 'It would be churlish to ignore the hedgehogs and, most of all, Toad.'

'Pooh, there's no knowing when *they'll* be back with us,' said Rabbit. 'And in any case they've played no part in our adventures.'

Now Hare felt he must intervene. 'I think some of us here present could hardly be said to have played much more of a part than they have,' he said pointedly. The remark was not lost on any of the others, Rabbit included. He looked a little foolish.

'Well, well, that's as may be,' said Badger, smoothing things over. 'But I don't think any of us need to have particular qualifications to enjoy ourselves together.'

'Why don't we make it a double celebration?' suggested Vixen. 'To mark our survival through our first winter and also to rejoice at seeing our hibernating friends again.'

'I think that's an excellent idea, Vixen,' said Badger. 'Don't you, Fox?'

'I do. Incidentally, does anyone realize we've none of us thought of Adder?'

'Certainly a case of out of sight, out of mind,' Tawny Owl remarked. 'But then, he's never the most genial of characters.'

'Nevertheless, it would be unthinkable not to have him with us,' Badger declared. 'In his own way, he's been a loyal enough friend.'

'As I have cause to remember,' murmured Vixen.

'Then it's postponed until the spring?' Weasel summarized.

'Perhaps not quite that long,' said Fox. 'The first

really mild spell will bring the hedgehogs out. And probably Toad, too. I'm not exactly sure how long snakes need to sleep.'

As February progressed to its conclusion, the final traces of snow and ice disappeared completely from the Park. The long, hard winter, which had begun so early, released its grip at last. Everything pointed to the fact that a warm spring was approaching, perhaps sooner than usual. Mild breezes blew and, underfoot, the ground was soft and spongy with water where the snow had melted. Most days were blessed with sunshine, however, which prevented the Reserve from becoming too waterlogged.

Already the earliest buds were swelling when the hedgehogs climbed out of their beds of thick leaves and twigs. Their first thought was food, and insects, slugs and spiders were in such abundance because of the mild weather, that they could never have guessed that for months previously their friends had battled against starvation. The hedgehogs' elected leader, having feasted grandly, went to look for signs of his old travelling companions.

As always, Kestrel was the first to spot this new movement on the ground. He dived downwards to intercept his recently emerged friend. 'Hallo, Hedgehog! Hallo!' he called as he hurtled down.

'Kestrel! It's good to see you!' said Hedgehog enthusiastically. 'How have you been?'

'Better than most,' Kestrel informed him. 'How did you sleep?'

Hedgehog laughed. 'Like a log – as always,' he replied. 'And the others? Have they fared well?'

'Not all of them, I'm afraid. You have been well out of the troubles we've experienced since we last saw you.'

'Dear, dear,' said Hedgehog. 'Has it been a bad winter, then?'

'The worst any of us can remember,' answered Kestrel. 'And that includes Badger.'

'But tell me,' Hedgehog said, looking concerned, 'have any lost their lives?'

'Many,' said the hawk simply. 'The voles are reduced to a single pair – Vole himself and his mate – and the fieldmice only one better. The rabbits have suffered badly, too. And the squirrels have had their losses.'

'This is shocking,' responded Hedgehog. 'I never expected anything like this. But Fox, Badger, Vixen . . .?'

'The larger animals have all survived – but only just. I tell you, Hedgehog, you can't conceive how near to death we all were. I think this winter has left its mark on everyone.'

'Is little Mole then – ?'

'No, no. He's all right. I think he suffered less than anyone. It appears his beloved worms are easier to find in cold weather – it restricts their movements.'

Hedgehog nodded. 'And the other birds?'

'Yes, Owl and Whistler have made it, too. But the winter hasn't been the only thing we've had to contend with.'

'Good gracious! What else?'

'Well, come along. Come and see the others and you'll hear all about it. I'll meet you at Badger's set.'

So Hedgehog made his way along and soon was surrounded by a number of the other animals. Together they told him of the harrowing events during the preceding months. At the end of it, he felt glad and relieved that *some* of his friends were there to greet him.

'And I've slept through it all in blissful ignorance,' he said wonderingly.

'Best thing to have done,' Hare told him. 'You've had a happy release.'

With the re-appearance of the hedgehogs, the animals knew that their party, although reduced, would soon be together again. One particularly warm morning in early March they all decided to make the trip to the Pond, as Badger was quite convinced that Toad and Adder would be tempted by its pleasantness from their burrow.

As they approached the water, the scene of such a dramatic occurrence during the winter, there were already signs of activity. The Edible Frogs had woken and were splashing about furiously, or sitting by the water's edge, croaking. And nearby, on a sunny slope, basking delightedly in the warm rays of the sun, who should they find but Adder?

'Mmmm,' he murmured dreamily as he spied the company, 'don't talk to me. I'm not really awake yet.'

The animals laughed but ignored his request.

'Certainly not alert,' Fox corrected him, referring to his proximity to the frogs, 'but definitely awake.'

'Where's Toad?' Badger asked. 'Did you leave him behind?'

'Oh no,' drawled Adder. 'When I awoke the hole was quite empty. He must have decided to greet the sun before me.'

'I wonder where he is,' said Badger. 'We couldn't have missed him.'

'I've no idea,' said the snake. 'But please – leave me. Let me doze.'

'Unsociable old so-and-so,' muttered Tawny Owl. 'We'll get no sense out of him for the moment.'

Fox was looking for the patriarch of the Pond, the large frog that knew Toad best. Perhaps he could throw some light on Toad's absence. He found him, newly glistening, surveying the scene from a piece of flat rock.

'Oh yes, I saw him,' he answered in reply to Fox's question. 'Two days ago. He was making off towards the Park boundary.'

'*What*!?'

'Yes – there, in that direction.'

The animals were stunned. What could he be up to?

'Perhaps he's lost his memory,' piped up Mole. 'During his long sleep, I mean,' he added, thinking he may have sounded silly.

'You all seem to have lost yours,' rejoined Adder in his lazy lisp. 'It's obvious what's happened. It's Spring. Toad's returning to his birthplace.' His red eyes glinted in the sun as he looked at their astonished faces contemptuously. 'He's on his way back to Farthing Wood.'

—20—

Whistled Off

The rest of the animals and the birds were dumbfounded. They looked at each other with blank faces. It was too incredible. Yet it had happened before. They all owed their knowledge of the Park's existence to Toad, who had discovered it and travelled across country for the best part of a year to bring news of it to the beleaguered Farthing Wood. On that occasion, however, he had been returning to his old home – Farthing Pond – only to find it had disappeared; destroyed by humans.

'But *this* is Toad's home now,' said Squirrel. 'He led us here. His old home no longer exists. How can he have forgotten all that?'

'I think he can't help himself,' observed Kestrel. 'It's his homing instinct. In the Spring it's like an irresistible

urge that draws Toad and creatures like him back to
their birthplace to spawn and reproduce themselves.
And Toad's birthplace was Farthing Pond.'

'It's quite true,' agreed Tawny Owl. 'None of us can
forget when, on our journey here, Toad started doubling
back because the pull of his old home was still so strong.'

'Well, he can't have gone far,' said Fox. 'Not in two
days. We must find him and reason with him.'

'No time like the present,' said Badger. 'He may not
even have left the Reserve yet.'

'I'll see if I can spot him,' Kestrel offered. 'But his
camouflage is so good it might be difficult.'

'There's no need for us all to go,' said Fox. 'That
would only delay things. Badger and I will go with
Vixen and, Whistler, perhaps you can assist Kestrel in
the search?'

'I shall be delighted to do anything in my power,' said
the heron, flapping his wings and making his familiar
whistling noise.

'We'll visit you again, Adder,' Fox told the still mo-
tionless snake. 'I hope by then our party will be
complete.'

'You can visit if you wish,' replied Adder. 'But I can't
guarantee to be in the same spot. I have other things to
do apart from lying around here waiting for your return.'

'Ungracious as ever,' said Tawny Owl loudly, but
Adder was quite used to such remarks and only flicked
his forked tongue in and out in a derogatory manner.

While the other animals dispersed, the two foxes and
Badger trotted off in the direction of the Hollow. It was
here they had all spent their first night on arriving in
White Deer Park, and it was close to the hole in the
fence through which they had first entered. Fox was
quite sure Toad would be travelling on the same route
if he had, indeed, intended to leave the Reserve.

Fox and Vixen skirted the Hollow while Badger entered it to make quite certain Toad was not safely there, all the time waiting for his friends at the traditional meeting-point. But he was not, and when they arrived at the boundary on this side of the Park they found Kestrel waiting for them.

'No sign as yet,' he announced. 'I think he must be outside.'

'What a nuisance he is,' said Badger. 'Now we'll all be exposing ourselves to risk on his behalf.'

'It's obvious we can't stay together outside the Park,' said Fox. 'We shall be far too conspicuous. But he can't possibly be far away, travelling at his pace. Kestrel, can you scout around in the immediate area for a bit? He may only be a matter of a few paces away.'

But when Kestrel alighted again the answer was the same. Whistler, too, had had no luck. 'There seems to be a distinct dearth of toads in the area,' he informed them in his droll way.

'There's nothing for it, then,' said Fox, 'but that we'll have to go through the fence. We'll split up and try a separate patch each.'

'Wouldn't it be wiser for you to leave it until nightfall?' suggested Kestrel.

'Safer, yes,' admitted Fox. 'But more difficult. Toad is a small animal and would be even harder to locate in the dark.'

'We'll keep our eyes open for you all, then,' said Kestrel. 'And we can warn you if necessary.'

'Thanks,' said Fox. 'Well, Vixen, Badger, shall we go?'

The three animals passed singly through the broken fence and Fox allotted them each their areas. 'If you find him,' he said to them, 'make the birds understand and they can round up the other two of us.'

So they each went their different ways, using sight and scent in their search.

It was Vixen in the end who found their lost friend. Perhaps half a mile from where she left the Park a narrow and normally shallow little brook ran bubbling across country. On its banks sat two small boys watching the water – now swollen by the thaw – run gurgling past them. Occasionally they would dip their nets into the stream, for they were collecting sticklebacks and water-bugs and anything else that came along. By their side on the bank were some big jars full of water into which they were emptying their nets whenever they caught a new specimen. All this Vixen saw as she approached as close as she could before having to hide herself among some gorse scrub. From this vantage point she could watch securely and see everything. What she saw in one of the jars made her heart skip a beat. For it was a toad, and she knew that, as likely as not, it was her toad. But then she was not so sure, for another of the jars also contained a toad, and this one was considerably larger than the other.

The two poor entombed creatures were jumping up and down in the water inside the jars, banging their blunt noses against the glass in frenzied and utterly useless attempts to escape. Their exit was firmly sealed by metal lids. Now Vixen was in a dilemma. For there was nothing she could do to free the toads. Yet she knew she must prevent the boys taking the jars away with them before she knew if her friend was one of the captives. She certainly needed Fox's advice and as quickly as possible, because the boys might choose to leave at any time.

From the safety of the gorse-bushes she barked, hoping one of the birds might be close. She saw the boys look up at the noise, and peer all about them. But they could see nothing, and soon turned their attention to the stream again.

Neither Kestrel nor Whistler heard Vixen's call, but Whistler had seen the stream and the boys while on the wing and now came looking for the three animals to warn them of the presence of humans. Luckily, as Vixen was closest, he found her first.

'I've seen them,' she nodded as he landed awkwardly beside her. 'And I think I've seen Toad.'

'Perfect!' cried the heron. 'Then we can collect him and make a hasty retreat.'

'It's not as simple as that, I'm afraid, Whistler,' she answered, and explained what was in the glass jars.

'How awful! Whatever can we do?' he boomed.

'I don't know. But you must bring Fox. He'll think of something. And tell Badger, too.'

'At once,' said the heron and flapped noisily into flight again. Vixen shuddered as she saw his huge form rise above her, immediately catching the attention of the two fascinated little humans who began to point and chatter excitedly. Fortunately, however, they did not move from the stream bank.

Fox and Badger came quietly and cautiously to join Vixen behind her prickly screen. They listened to her news.

'Of course it may not be Toad,' said Fox, 'but, naturally, we can't take the chance.'

'Oh dear, oh dear,' said Badger anxiously. 'Poor creatures. This is just the same way he was captured in Farthing Pond and brought all this way from his home.'

'A blessing in disguise, as it turned out,' Fox reminded him. 'Otherwise there would have been no White Deer Park for *us*.'

'I know, I know,' Badger nodded. 'But it is no blessing this time.'

'Well, there's only one thing to do,' declared Fox resolutely. 'We must rescue both these toads.'

'Of course. But how?'

'We'll take the captors by surprise. They're young. They may scare easily. If we all rush on them together, barking and snarling, they may run. To take them by surprise is our only hope. Hallo, here's Kestrel!'

Whistler had also informed Kestrel of developments. No sooner had he heard than the hawk had flown close to the brook, hovering as he examined the jars' contents with his phenomenal eye power. He came swooping up to the three animals. 'One of them is Toad all right,' he screeched. 'The smaller one.'

'Get Whistler back here,' Fox ordered peremptorily. 'I have need of his great bill.'

The heron came wheeling low to listen to the plan.

'As we make our charge you must sail in and snatch the jar up in your bill. Make sure it's the one with the smaller of the two toads inside,' Fox told him. 'Right, all ready? Together then!'

Across the grass hurtled Fox, Badger and Vixen making the utmost racket possible. The two boys jumped up, uncertain what to do. As they hesitated Whistler soared over and plummeted downward like a dive bomber. Barely giving himself time to land, he snatched at a jar and lumbered away, surprised at the object's weight. The boys seized the other jars, including the one containing the second toad, and made off along the bank, leaving their nets behind as the fierce animals approached them. Then Fox, Badger and Vixen heard Kestrel screaming at Whistler in the air. 'It's the wrong jar! You've got the wrong one!'

Partly in alarm and partly because his bill was already aching dreadfully at the unaccustomed weight, Whistler let go of the jar, which crashed to the ground and in-

stantly shattered. Out jumped the strange toad, none
the worse for the experience, having been buoyed up by
the water. 'Thank you! Thank you!' it called in its croaky
voice and began to hop away as fast as its legs could
carry it.

Now Whistler felt he must atone for his error. He
came sailing back after the frightened boys and stabbed
at them with his pointed beak, with the idea of making
them drop Toad. So vicious were his attacks that this
ploy met with quick success. All the jars were dropped
by the shrieking boys, the one carrying Toad rolling
down the bank and landing with a plop in the stream.
There it was buffeted and swept along by the current,
the jar pivoting end to end as it spun away.

Inside the jar Toad was stunned, dazed, stupefied.
One minute the jar had been standing on end on the
bank, then it had been grabbed up in the air and he had
bobbed up and down while the boy ran with it; then it
had fallen with a thud to the ground, rolled over and
over and now was racing along on the water, the reeds
and rushes shooting past on either side of his clear glass
prison. He did not know that any of his friends were
involved in the events, for all had happened too quickly.
The next thing he knew the jar came to rest against a
submerged barrier in the water. He looked out of the
glass and saw two stilt-like legs pressed against the side.
Then down came a huge beak and Toad, jar and all,
was hoisted up, higher and higher and higher still into
the sky.

'Don't drop him!' shouted Fox. 'Carry him to the
Park!'

'And back to the Park with us!' cried Badger. 'The
party is complete!'

——— 21 ———
Home or Away?

Once safely inside the Park fence again, the five friends
made for the Hollow. Whistler carefully deposited the
jar on the ground and they all stood looking at it. By
now Toad had recognized the faces and was leaping
about desperately.

'Now what do we do?' Kestrel queried. Whistler was
resting his aching beak and was unable to speak. The
three animals stared at Toad and frowned. Toad settled
down and stared back.

Eventually Whistler said, 'The other toad came to no
harm when I dropped it. May I suggest a repeat
performance?'

Fox shook his head. 'No. We can't risk it. The other

toad was lucky not to have been cut by the glass. But it
may not be such a lucky drop again.'

'Well, I'm afraid if that lid doesn't come off soon,
Toad might suffocate,' Badger said worriedly. 'We don't
know how long he's been in there.'

'What if we found a large stone and dropped it on the
jar?' Kestrel suggested.

'Who could carry such a stone?' Fox asked. 'And it
would be even more dangerous for Toad inside.'

'I think there's only one way he'll get out of there,'
Vixen said.

'Well, Vixen, what is it?' Fox asked quickly.

'The Warden,' she replied.

'Bravo!' cried Badger. 'We'll take the jar to him. He
can open it.'

'Well, Counsellor, you've done it again,' Fox smiled
at her. 'Whistler, are you up to portering a little further?'

'The heart is always willing, my dear Fox. But my
poor bill does the carrying,' he answered. 'However, if
it's a case of life and death. . . .'

'I'm afraid it is,' said Fox. 'We'll meet you at the
cottage.'

So once again the baffled and desperate Toad was
hoisted into the air, and once again the ground rushed
away from beneath him. The next time he was set down
he was terrified to see a cat's face come and peer at him,
and he became more frantic than ever. Whistler stood
by the side of the jar enigmatically. His large size made
him quite fearless of the Warden's pet. He knew Fox,
Badger and Vixen would be a long time arriving for,
even without snow on the ground, the journey was a
considerable one. Kestrel discreetly stayed well out of
the way.

'Whatever have you got here?' Ginger Cat whispered,
prowling all round the container.

'An old friend of mine,' answered Whistler, 'who's got himself into a spot of bother.'

'He has, hasn't he? He won't get out of there very easily.'

'Not on his own, no. Is your master within?'

'I have no – ' Ginger Cat began, then shrugged. 'I believe so,' he finished. 'I see now. You want his assistance. Bring that object outside the door, and I'll try to attract his attention.'

Whistler complied, and Ginger Cat commenced an almighty howling outside the cottage door. There was no response. 'I'll have to fetch him,' he said, and squeezed through the cat flap. Whistler heard more miaowing and wailing going on inside and then, at last, the door opened. Ginger Cat stepped daintily out, followed by a puzzled Warden.

The man looked down and saw a sedentary heron guarding a large glass jar with something inside it. He did not know what to make of such a sight. Whistler decided to give him a clue. 'Kraaank,' he cried raucously, and pushed the jar towards the man's feet. The man bent and picked up the jar and saw the toad inside. Whistler snapped his bill excitedly, producing a sound like a castanet. The man looked at him and looked back at the jar. He knew herons ate creatures like frogs and could only surmise it had discovered this titbit and could not get at it. He unscrewed the lid and gently tipped Toad out, intending to save him from the two predators at hand. But before he could pick up the small creature, Toad leapt away as fast as he could, making for cover.

Ginger Cat saw the movement and made as if to pounce. But Whistler forestalled him. 'Leave it all to me, Toad, my friend,' he said and carefully lowered his beak. The Warden watched enthralled as the heron, instead of gobbling the morsel straight down its gullet as he had expected, gently took it up and flew away into the centre of the Park.

Fox, Badger and Vixen saw Whistler coming, carrying Toad, and ceased to run. Then they made a circle round Toad as he put his feet hesitantly on the ground, and gave him encouraging licks.

'Dear old Toad,' said Badger, almost overcome. 'What an adventure you've had! Oh, it's good to have you safe with us.'

'Thank you, Badger, thank you,' said Toad. 'And, Whistler, thank you most of all. I never thought I would see any of you again.'

'Why did you do it? Why did you leave the Park?' Fox asked. 'We came looking for you this morning at the Pond and Adder said you had gone.'

'I just can't stop myself, Fox,' Toad answered. 'I know it's silly, but in the spring I feel I have to go home. I seem to lose all control over myself. It's like being taken over by some kind of Power, much greater and stronger than I am.'

'But this is your home now,' said Badger. 'There *is* no other home for you. Your birthplace no longer exists.'

'I know. I know it. But I *have* to go.'

'Well, you see what happens when you stray outside the safety of the Reserve,' Fox admonished him. 'You're lucky to be back here.'

'Oh, don't you think I know it? You're all so sensible. Everything you say is true. You'll have to restrain me.'

'Perhaps we should have kept you in the jar until you can see sense,' Badger said and laughed.

'If only Adder had been awake when I woke,' Toad said, 'he might have dissuaded me. Oh, it's wonderful to see you all. Where are the others? Are they all right?'

'Not all of them,' Vixen said quietly. 'It was a cruel

winter, Toad. Some of your friends are no longer around to welcome you back.'

'But – but – surely – ' he stammered, 'there are – more – than just – you four?'

'Oh *yes*,' Fox said reassuringly. 'You've already seen Kestrel. And there's Mole and Hare and his family – well, less one actually – and *most* of the rabbits and squirrels and Weasel, of course. And Tawny Owl – he's indestructible.'

'And all the mice?'

'Er – no, not all. Well, not many, really. They took it the hardest.'

'The hedgehogs?'

'Yes, yes, the hedgehogs are all right. They slept through it all, just like you and Adder.'

'And then, Toad, off you were going to go without even coming to see if we were still alive?' Badger said pointedly.

'Oh, Badger! I feel so guilty,' said the wretched animal. 'How could I? Never to know what you've all suffered!'

His friends fell silent as they watched Toad's anguish.

Badger, compassionate as always, spoke first. 'What can we do to help?' he asked.

'I don't know,' croaked Toad miserably. 'Except not to let me out of your sight – at least until the mating season's over.'

'Well, well, perhaps we can keep shifts,' Badger said jokingly.

'We've a lot more to tell you about our months without you,' said Fox. 'And Adder hasn't heard the tale yet. You'll both want to meet up with all the others again, won't you? I think we should all meet in the Hollow just like we used to. We haven't all been together since last autumn.'

'An excellent idea,' agreed Badger. 'We must pass the word. Er – Toad, I want you to stay with me for the time being. For safety's sake, you know. Would you care to climb on my back?'

While his friends had been thus occupied, Kestrel had continued in his usual pastime of skimming over the Reserve on effortless wings, soaring and diving again. But he saw something that made him drop earthwards in curiosity. Through the gap in the fence where Fox, Badger and Vixen had recently passed in and out of the Park now came a solitary, plump toad – the very one Whistler had rescued and then dropped. Kestrel landed and spoke to the stranger.

'Are you seeking sanctuary here now?' he asked. 'You'd be wise to do so.'

'In a way,' replied the toad. 'This is my home. I was born here in the pond. It's spring and I've been travelling towards it since I came out of hibernation. During the summer I wander quite a way and last winter I hibernated outside the Park.'

Kestrel was struck by the irony of the opposing directions Toad and the stranger had taken to return to their respective birthplaces, meeting in the middle, as it were, by the brook-side. 'How strange,' he murmured. The toad gave him a quizzical look which prompted him to explain.

'Yes, that is the way of things,' said the toad. 'We didn't speak. I was already in a jar when the young humans caught your friend. I believe he'd been swimming in the stream.'

'So you are returning to mate?' Kestrel asked.

'Yes. I'm full of spawn at this time of year,' replied the toad, revealing that she was a female. 'When I'm paired the eggs will be released in the water and fertilized by my mate.'

Kestrel glared at the toad. An idea had struck him. 'I beg your pardon,' he said. 'I'm not an expert on amphibia. I hadn't realized you are a lady toad. What are you called?'

'Paddock,' she replied.

'I'm delighted to have had this talk,' said Kestrel. 'And I think our friend will be interested to hear about it.'

'May I say how grateful I am for my rescue,' said Paddock. 'Now my babies will be born in safety.'

'I hope we may meet again,' the hawk said courteously. 'But now I'll leave you to continue your journey.' He spread his wings again.

In the air he floated blissfully on warm currents, thinking hard. Unexpectedly, he had perhaps discovered the one thing that might keep Toad in White Deer Park. The pull of Farthing Pond could perhaps be surmounted by Toad's desire for a mate.

22
Life Goes On

No sooner had Kestrel come to this conclusion than he
went in search of Fox, who told him that Toad had been
restored to them. The hawk described his discussion
with Paddock and asked Fox's opinion of his idea.

'Kestrel, I really think you've hit upon something,' he
replied. 'After all, the sole reason for these journeys of
toads and frogs to their home ponds is to breed. We'll
introduce a dash of romance into our friend's life.'

'Where *is* Toad?' asked Kestrel. 'Perhaps we should
intercept Paddock's journey to the pond before any other
male shows interest.'

'A good point,' acknowledged Fox. 'Come on. He's
with Badger.'

'By the set they found Toad talking to an excited

Mole. Badger was doing the rounds of the Farthing Wood animals, now back in their individual homes, to tell them of the meeting in the Hollow.

'Isn't it grand to have Toad back?' Mole chattered. 'It's just like old times.'

'Did Badger get tired of carrying you?' Fox asked Toad with a grin.

'He made me get down,' Toad said ruefully. 'He said I was tugging at his coat so. It's my grasping pads, you see.' He held up his horny front feet, one at a time, to demonstrate. 'They become very developed at this time of year. That's so that we males can hang on tight to our mates and not get separated.'

'Well, I think we can find something else for you to grasp on to,' said Fox, delighted that Toad had unwittingly introduced the subject himself. 'But first, you must hang on to me.'

'Now it really is like old times,' chuckled Toad. 'Remember how you used to carry me on our journey here, Fox?'

'Of course I do,' said Fox. 'Now, up you get. Ouch!' He winced. 'I see what Badger means. Ow! Well really, Toad, you didn't grip as hard as this even when I rescued you from the fire.'

'I'm sorry,' said Toad. 'I'll try not to tug too much. Where are we going?'

'Wait and see,' was the mysterious reply. 'Now, Kestrel, which way please?'

The lady toad had not progressed very far into the Park. She had paused to refresh herself with some insects and seemed to have settled down to digest them.

Toad dismounted of his own accord by leaping from Fox's back. 'My, what a beauty!' he exclaimed as he saw Paddock. He looked at Fox with a wry grin that seemed to express better than words what he thought of his friend. Fox grinned back and only stayed long enough to see Toad grasp the unprotesting Paddock firmly round her middle. He was amused to see how much larger than Toad she was as she waddled off with her affectionate burden on her way to the Pond.

'Well I never,' Fox laughed to himself. 'And not a word exchanged! I wonder how Vixen would like me to be so matter of fact?'

Kestrel also had been watching from the air. 'I thought so,' he muttered. 'Easy as pie.'

Some days later Adder was seen sunning himself in the Hollow.

'Hallo, stranger!' cried Weasel. 'We've all been waiting for you to put in an appearance. We're having a get-together.'

'Very nice, I'm sure,' remarked Adder. 'But you are mistaken if you believe I came to this spot out of any gregarious tendency. The fact is I could no longer witness the shameless scenes in that Pond with equanimity.'

'What *are* you talking about, Adder?'

'The length and breadth of the water is alive with courting couples,' he replied, 'whether they be frogs, toads or newts.'

'Well, naturally – it's Spring,' said Weasel. 'Or hadn't you realized?'

'I'm quite aware of that,' Adder snapped. 'But they seem to have no regard at all for others in the area with the way they're carrying on. Even Toad has been affected by it,' he added primly.

'This sounds to me like a touch of jealousy,' Weasel remarked pointedly.

'Rubbish,' returned Adder. 'It's not a touch of anything except perhaps good breeding.'

'More like a lack of breeding, in your case,' Weasel rejoined wickedly.

'If you'll excuse me, I don't care to converse in this manner,' Adder told him, and began to slither away.

'Don't go!' cried Weasel, who now regretted his unkind remark. 'I didn't mean what I said. I'm sorry. Please stay. We hardly ever see you.'

Adder, never very susceptible to overtures of friendship, flickered his tongue in an uncertain manner. He hated to give signs of weakness. In the end he compromised. 'I'm going on a hunting trip,' he told Weasel. 'I haven't eaten for five months. But when I've managed to put a little plumpness behind my scales I'll be back.'

Weasel had to be content with this vague promise, and went to convey it to the rest of the community.

'Well, at least he doesn't intend to shun us completely,' said Fox.

'Best thing for him to do is to hunt himself up a nice female adder,' Tawny Owl observed crustily. 'She would take some of the starchiness out of him.'

'Isn't he a character, though?' Vixen laughed. 'He really is quite unique.'

'Thank goodness for that,' said Hare. 'Just imagine two like him around.'

'So it seems as if our celebration is to be delayed once more?' said Badger. 'I wonder when Toad will leave the Pond?'

'Not till the mating season's over,' answered Fox, glancing a little coyly at Vixen. 'And we know how long that goes on.'

Back in White Deer Pond, Toad and Paddock were still united as she dived underwater to lay her eggs. Other toads had already done so, for strings of eggs could be seen wound round weed and plant-stem. But the offspring of Toad and Paddock were destined to start their tadpole life in a different setting. For these eggs, as they descended in the water, attached themselves to some very different objects sticking up from the mud: the rusting remains of two quite harmless shotguns.

At last the day dawned when all the animals were ready to hold their celebration. Fox and Vixen made their way to the Hollow where many of their friends had already gathered. They could see Badger and Weasel chatting lightheartedly with Kestrel, while Hare and Rabbit exchanged views from the midst of their families. Toad, Adder and Tawny Owl had assembled on the lip of the Hollow and looked towards the pair of foxes as if awaiting their arrival.

'Dear, dear friends,' murmured Fox. 'How glad I am to see them together again. I think we should count our blessings that so many of us are still here to take pleasure in each other's company.'

'Yes, indeed,' said Vixen. 'It's due to our ties of friendship more than anything else that we were able to survive our troubles. Alone, it could have been another story.'

Fox nodded. Now they could see the smaller animals bunching together in a corner of their meeting-place. Mole was there with the mice, the squirrels and the hedgehogs. In the air a familiar whistle heralded the arrival of their friend the heron.

'A fond greeting to you all,' said Whistler joyfully as he landed amongst the sprouting bracken. 'This is a wonderful day!'

'Then let's make it one we shall always remember,' said Fox. 'So that, whatever may happen in the future, whatever fate may befall us, we shall remember that this day, together, we rejoiced to say that WE ARE ALIVE.'